A DARK NIGHT'S WORK

By

Elizabeth Gaskell

CHAPTER I.

In the county town of a certain shire there lived (about forty years ago) one Mr. Wilkins, a conveyancing attorney of considerable standing.

The certain shire was but a small county, and the principal town in it contained only about four thousand inhabitants; so in saying that Mr. Wilkins was the principal lawyer in Hamley, I say very little, unless I add that he transacted all the legal business of the gentry for twenty miles round. His grandfather had established the connection; his father had consolidated and strengthened it, and, indeed, by his wise and upright conduct, as well as by his professional skill, had obtained for himself the position of confidential friend to many of the surrounding families of distinction. He visited among them in a way which no mere lawyer had ever done before; dined at their tables—he alone, not accompanied by his wife, be it observed; rode to the meet occasionally as if by accident, although he was as well mounted as any squire among them, and was often persuaded (after a little coquetting about "professional engagements," and "being wanted at the office") to have a run with his clients; nay, once or twice he forgot his usual caution, was first in at the death, and rode home with the brush. But in general he knew his place; as his place was held to be in that aristocratic county, and in those days. Nor let be supposed that he was in any way a toadeater. He respected himself too much for that. He would give the most unpalatable advice, if need were; would counsel an unsparing reduction of expenditure to an extravagant man; would recommend such an abatement of family pride as paved the way for one or two happy marriages in some instances; nay, what was the most likely piece of conduct of all to give offence forty years ago, he would speak up for an unjustly-used tenant; and that with so much temperate and well-timed wisdom and good feeling, that he more than once gained his point. He had one son, Edward. This boy was the secret joy and pride of his father's heart. For himself he was not in the least ambitious, but it did cost him a hard struggle to acknowledge that his own business was too lucrative, and brought in too large an income, to pass away into the hands of a stranger, as it would do if he indulged his ambition for his son by giving him a college education and making him into a barrister. This determination on the more prudent side of the argument took place while Edward was at Eton. The lad had, perhaps, the largest allowance of pocket-money of any boy at school; and he had always looked forward to going to Christ Church along with his fellows, the sons of the squires, his father's employers. It was a severe mortification to him to find that his destiny was changed, and that he had to return to Hamley to be articled to his father, and to assume the hereditary subservient position to lads whom he had licked in the play-ground, and beaten at learning.

His father tried to compensate him for the disappointment by every indulgence which money could purchase. Edward's horses were even finer than those of his father; his literary tastes were kept up and fostered, by his father's permission to form an extensive library, for which purpose a noble room was added to Mr. Wilkins's already extensive house in the suburbs of Hamley. And after his year of legal study in London his father sent him to make the grand tour, with something very like carte blanche as to expenditure, to judge from the packages which were sent home from various parts of the Continent.

At last he came home—came back to settle as his father's partner at Hamley. He was a son to be proud of, and right down proud was old Mr. Wilkins of his handsome, accomplished, gentlemanly lad. For Edward was not one to be spoilt by the course of indulgence he had passed through; at least, if it had done him an injury, the effects were at present hidden from view. He had no vulgar vices; he was, indeed, rather too refined for the society he was likely to be thrown into, even supposing that society to consist of the highest of his father's employers. He was well read, and an artist of no mean pretensions. Above all, "his heart was in the right place," as his father used to observe. Nothing could exceed the deference he always showed to him. His mother had long been dead.

I do not know whether it was Edward's own ambition or his proud father's wishes that had led him to attend the Hamley assemblies. I should conjecture the latter, for Edward had of himself too much good taste to wish to intrude into any society. In the opinion of all the shire, no society had more reason to consider itself select than that which met at every full moon in the Hamley assembly-room, an excrescence built on to the principal inn in the town by the joint subscription of all the county families. Into those choice and mysterious precincts no towns person was ever allowed to enter; no professional man might set his foot therein; no infantry officer saw the interior of that ball, or that card-room. The old original subscribers would fain have had a man prove his sixteen quarterings before he might make his bow to the queen of the night; but the old original founders of the Hamley assemblies were dropping off; minuets had vanished with them, country dances had died away; quadrilles were in high vogue—nay, one or two of the high magnates of ---shire were trying to introduce waltzing, as they had seen it in London, where it had come in with the visit of the allied sovereigns, when Edward Wilkins made his *début* on these boards. He had been at many splendid assemblies abroad, but still the little old ballroom attached to the George Inn in his native town was to him a place grander and more awful than the most magnificent saloons he had seen in Paris or Rome. He laughed at himself for this unreasonable feeling of awe; but there it was notwithstanding. He had been dining at the house of one of the lesser gentry, who was under considerable obligations to his father, and who was the parent of eight "muckle-mou'ed" daughters, so hardly likely to oppose much aristocratic resistance to the elder Mr. Wilkins's clearly implied wish that Edward should be presented at the Hamley assembly-rooms. But many a squire glowered and looked black at the introduction of Wilkins the attorney's son into the sacred precincts; and perhaps there would have been much more mortification than pleasure in this assembly to the young man, had it not been for an incident that occurred pretty late in the evening. The lord-lieutenant of the county usually came with a large party to the Hamley assemblies once in a season; and this night he was expected, and with him a fashionable duchess and her daughters. But time wore on, and they did not make their appearance. At last there was a rustling and a bustling, and in sailed the superb party. For a few minutes dancing was stopped; the earl led the duchess to a sofa; some of their acquaintances came up to speak to them; and then the quadrilles were finished in rather a flat manner. A country dance followed, in which none of the lord-lieutenant's party joined; then there was a consultation, a request, an inspection of the dancers, a message to the orchestra, and the band struck up a waltz; the duchess's daughters flew off to the music, and some more young ladies seemed ready to follow, but, alas! there was a lack of gentlemen acquainted with the new-fashioned dance. One of the stewards bethought him of young Wilkins, only just returned from the Continent. Edward was a beautiful dancer, and waltzed to admiration. For his next partner he had one of the Lady ---s; for the duchess, to whom the—shire squires and their little county politics and contempts were alike unknown, saw no reason why her lovely Lady Sophy should not have a good partner, whatever his pedigree might be, and begged the stewards to introduce Mr. Wilkins to her. After this night his fortune was made with the young ladies of the Hamley assemblies. He was not unpopular with the mammas; but the heavy squires still looked at him askance, and the heirs (whom he had licked at Eton) called him an upstart behind his back.

CHAPTER II.

It was not a satisfactory situation. Mr. Wilkins had given his son an education and tastes beyond his position. He could not associate with either profit or pleasure with the doctor or the brewer of Hamley; the vicar was old and deaf, the curate a raw young man, half frightened at the sound of his own voice. Then, as to matrimony—for the idea of his marriage was hardly more present in Edward's mind than in that of his father—he could scarcely fancy bringing home any one of the young ladies of Hamley to the elegant mansion, so full of suggestion and association to an educated person, so inappropriate a dwelling for an ignorant, uncouth, ill-brought-up girl. Yet Edward was fully aware, if his fond father was not, that of all the young ladies who were glad enough of him as a partner at the Hamley assemblies, there was not of them but would have considered herself affronted by an offer of marriage from an attorney, the son and grandson of attorneys. The young man had perhaps received many a slight and mortification pretty quietly during these years, which yet told upon his character in after life. Even at this very time they were having their effect. He was of too sweet a disposition to show resentment, as many men would have done. But nevertheless he took a secret pleasure in the power which his father's money gave him. He would buy an expensive horse after five minutes' conversation as to the price, about which a needy heir of one of the proud county families had been haggling for three weeks. His dogs were from the best kennels in England, no matter at what cost; his guns were the newest and most improved make; and all these were expenses on objects which were among those of daily envy to the squires and squires' sons around. They did not much care for the treasures of art, which report said were being accumulated in Mr. Wilkins's house. But they did covet the horses and hounds he possessed, and the young man knew that they coveted, and rejoiced in it.

By-and-by he formed a marriage, which went as near as marriages ever do towards pleasing everybody. He was desperately in love with Miss Lamotte, so he was delighted when she consented to be his wife. His father was delighted in his delight, and, besides, was charmed to remember that Miss Lamotte's mother had been Sir Frank Holster's younger sister, and that, although her marriage had been disowned by her family, as beneath her in rank, yet no one could efface her name out of the Baronetage, where Lettice, youngest daughter of Sir Mark Holster, born 1772, married H. Lamotte, 1799, died 1810, was duly chronicled. She had left two children, a boy and a girl, of whom their uncle, Sir Frank, took charge, as their father was worse than dead—an outlaw whose name was never mentioned. Mark Lamotte was in the army; Lettice had a dependent position in her uncle's family; not intentionally made more dependent than was rendered necessary by circumstances, but still dependent enough to grate on the feelings of a sensitive girl, whose natural susceptibilty to slights was redoubled by the constant recollection of her father's disgrace. As Mr. Wilkins well knew, Sir Frank was considerably involved; but it was with very mixed feelings that he listened to the suit which would provide his penniless niece with a comfortable, not to say luxurious, home, and with a handsome, accomplished young man of unblemished character for a husband. He said one or two bitter and insolent things to Mr. Wilkins, even while he was giving his consent to the match; that was his temper, his proud, evil temper; but he really and permanently was satisfied with the connection, though he would occasionally turn round on his nephew-in-law, and sting him with a covert insult, as to his want of birth, and the inferior position which he held, forgetting, apparently, that his own brother-in-law and Lettice's father might be at any moment brought to the bar of justice if he attempted to re-enter his native country.

Edward was annoyed at all this; Lettice resented it. She loved her husband dearly, and was proud of him, for she had discernment enough to see how superior he was in every way to her cousins, the young Holsters, who borrowed his horses, drank his wines, and yet had caught their father's habit of sneering at his profession. Lettice wished that Edward would content himself with a purely domestic life, would let himself drop out of the company of the ---shire squirearchy, and find his relaxation with her, in their luxurious library, or lovely drawing-room, so full of white gleaming statues, and gems of pictures. But, perhaps, this was too much to expect of any man, especially of one who felt himself fitted in many ways to shine in society, and who was social by nature. Sociality in that county at that time meant conviviality. Edward did not care for wine, and yet he was obliged to drink—and by-and-by he grew to pique himself on his character as a judge of wine. His father by this time was dead; dead, happy old man, with a contented heart—his affairs flourishing, his poorer neighbours loving him, his richer respecting him, his son and daughter-in-law, the most affectionate and devoted that ever man had, and his healthy conscience at peace with his God.

Lettice could have lived to herself and her husband and children. Edward daily required more and more the stimulus of society. His wife wondered how he could care to accept dinner invitations from people who treated him as "Wilkins the attorney, a very good sort of fellow," as they introduced him to strangers who might be staying in the country, but who had no power to appreciate the taste, the talents, the impulsive artistic nature which she held so dear. She forgot that by accepting such invitations Edward was occasionally brought into contact with people not merely of high conventional, but of high intellectual rank; that when a certain amount of wine had dissipated his sense of inferiority of rank and position, he was a brilliant talker, a man to be listened to and admired even by wandering London statesmen, professional diners-out, or any great authors who might find themselves visitors in a ---shire country-house. What she would have had him share from the pride of her heart, she should have warned him to avoid from the temptations to sinful extravagance which it led him into. He had begun to spend more than he ought, not in intellectual—though that would have been wrong—but in purely sensual things. His wines, his table, should be such as no squire's purse or palate could command. His dinner-parties—small in number, the viands rare and delicate in quality, and sent up to table by an Italian cook—should be such as even the London stars should notice with admiration. He would have Lettice dressed in the richest materials, the most delicate lace; jewellery, he said, was beyond their means; glancing with proud humility at the diamonds of the elder ladies, and the alloyed gold of the younger. But he managed to spend as much on his wife's lace as would have bought many a set of inferior jewellery. Lettice well became it all. If as people said, her father had been nothing but a French adventurer, she bore traces of her nature in her grace, her delicacy, her fascinating and elegant ways of doing all things. She was made for society; and yet she hated it. And one day she went out of it altogether and for evermore. She had been well in the morning when Edward went down to his office in Hamley. At noon he was sent for by hurried trembling messengers. When he got home breathless and uncomprehending, she was past speech. One glance from her lovely loving black eyes showed that she recognised him with the passionate yearning that had been one of the characteristics of her love through life. There was no word passed between them. He could not speak, any more than could she. He knelt down by her. She was dying; she was dead; and he knelt on immovable. They brought him his eldest child, Ellinor, in utter despair what to do in order to rouse him. They had no thought as to the effect on her, hitherto shut up in the nursery during this busy day of confusion and alarm. The child had no idea of death, and her father, kneeling and tearless, was far less an object of surprise or interest to her than her mother, lying still and white, and not turning her head to smile at her darling.

"Mamma! mamma!" cried the child, in shapeless terror. But the mother never stirred; and the father hid his face yet deeper in the bedclothes, to stifle a cry as if a sharp knife had pierced his heart. The child forced her impetuous way from her attendants, and rushed to the bed. Undeterred by deadly cold or stony immobility, she kissed the lips and stroked the glossy raven hair, murmuring sweet words of wild love, such as had passed between the mother and child often and often when no witnesses were by; and altogether seemed so nearly beside herself in an agony of love and terror, that Edward arose, and softly taking her in his arms, bore her away, lying back like one dead (so exhausted was she by the terrible emotion they had forced on her childish heart), into his study, a little room opening out of the grand library, where on happy evenings, never to come again, he and his wife were wont to retire to have coffee together, and then perhaps stroll out of the glass-door into the open air, the shrubbery, the fields—never more to be trodden by those dear feet. What passed between father and child in this seclusion none could tell. Late in the evening Ellinor's supper was sent for, and the servant who brought it in saw the child lying as one dead in her father's arms, and before he left the room watched his master feeding her, the girl of six years of age, with as tender care as if she had been a baby of six months.

CHAPTER III.

From that time the tie between father and daughter grew very strong and tender indeed. Ellinor, it is true, divided her affection between her baby sister and her papa; but he, caring little for babies, had only a theoretic regard for his younger child, while the elder absorbed all his love. Every day that he dined at home Ellinor was placed opposite to him while he ate his late dinner; she sat where her mother had done during the meal, although she had dined and even supped some time before on the more primitive nursery fare. It was half pitiful, half amusing, to see the little girl's grave, thoughtful ways and modes of speech, as if trying to act up to the dignity of her place as her father's companion, till sometimes the little head nodded off to slumber in the middle of lisping some wise little speech. "Old-fashioned," the nurses called her, and prophesied that she would not live long in consequence of her old-fashionedness. But instead of the fulfilment of this prophecy, the fat bright baby was seized with fits, and was well, ill, and dead in a day! Ellinor's grief was something alarming, from its quietness and concealment. She waited till she was left—as she thought—alone at nights, and then sobbed and cried her passionate cry for "Baby, baby, come back to me—come back;" till every one feared for the health of the frail little girl whose childish affections had had to stand two such shocks. Her father put aside all business, all pleasure of every kind, to win his darling from her grief. No mother could have done more, no tenderest nurse done half so much as Mr. Wilkins then did for Ellinor.

If it had not been for him she would have just died of her grief. As it was, she overcame it—but slowly, wearily—hardly letting herself love anyone for some time, as if she instinctively feared lest all her strong attachments should find a sudden end in death. Her love—thus dammed up into a small space—at last burst its banks, and overflowed on her father. It was a rich reward to him for all his care of her, and he took delight—perhaps a selfish delight—in all the many pretty ways she perpetually found of convincing him, if he had needed conviction, that he was ever the first object with her. The nurse told him that half an hour or so before the earliest time at which he could be expected home in the evenings, Miss Ellinor began to fold up her doll's things and lull the inanimate treasure to sleep. Then she would sit and listen with an intensity of attention for his footstep. Once the nurse had expressed some wonder at the distance at which Ellinor could hear her father's approach, saying that she had listened and could not hear a sound, to which Ellinor had replied:

"Of course you cannot; he is not your papa!"

Then, when he went away in the morning, after he had kissed her, Ellinor would run to a certain window from which she could watch him up the lane, now hidden behind a hedge, now reappearing through an open space, again out of sight, till he reached a great old beech-tree, where for an instant more she saw him. And then she would turn away with a sigh, sometimes reassuring her unspoken fears by saying softly to herself,

"He will come again to-night."

Mr. Wilkins liked to feel his child dependent on him for all her pleasures. He was even a little jealous of anyone who devised a treat or conferred a present, the first news of which did not come from or through him.

At last it was necessary that Ellinor should have some more instruction than her good old nurse could give. Her father did not care to take upon himself the office of teacher, which he thought he foresaw would necessitate occasional blame, an occasional exercise of authority, which might possibly render him less idolized by his little girl; so he commissioned Lady Holster to choose out one among her many *protégées* for a governess to his daughter. Now, Lady Holster, who kept a sort of amateur county register-office, was only too glad to be made of use in this way; but when she inquired a little further as to the sort of person required, all she could extract from Mr. Wilkins was:

"You know the kind of education a lady should have, and will, I am sure, choose a governess for Ellinor better than I could direct you. Only, please, choose some one who will not marry me, and who will let Ellinor go on making my tea, and doing pretty much what she likes, for she is so good they need not try to make her better, only to teach her what a lady should know."

Miss Monro was selected—a plain, intelligent, quiet woman of forty—and it was difficult to decide whether she or Mr. Wilkins took the most pains to avoid each other, acting with regard to Ellinor, pretty much like the famous Adam and Eve in the weather-glass: when the one came out the other went in. Miss Monro had been tossed about and overworked quite enough in her life not to value the privilege and indulgence of her evenings to herself, her comfortable schoolroom, her quiet cozy teas, her book, or her letter-writing afterwards. By mutual agreement she did not interfere with Ellinor and her ways and occupations on the evenings when the girl had not her father for companion; and these occasions became more and more frequent as years passed on, and the deep shadow was lightened which the sudden death that had visited his household had cast over him. As I have said before, he was always a popular man at dinner-parties. His amount of intelligence and accomplishment was rare in ---shire, and if it required more wine than formerly to bring his conversation up to the desired point of range and brilliancy, wine was not an article spared or grudged at the county dinner-tables. Occasionally his business took him up to London. Hurried as these journeys might be, he never returned without a new game, a new toy of some kind, to "make home pleasant to his little maid," as he expressed himself.

He liked, too, to see what was doing in art, or in literature; and as he gave pretty extensive orders for anything he admired, he was almost sure to be followed down to Hamley by one or two packages or parcels, the arrival and opening of which began soon to form the pleasant epochs in Ellinor's grave though happy life.

The only person of his own standing with whom Mr. Wilkins kept up any intercourse in Hamley was the new clergyman, a bachelor, about his own age, a learned man, a fellow of his college, whose first claim on Mr. Wilkins's attention was the fact that he had been travelling-bachelor for his university, and had consequently been on the Continent about the very same two years that Mr. Wilkins had been there; and although they had never met, yet they had many common acquaintances and common recollections to talk over of this period, which, after all, had been about the most bright and hopeful of Mr. Wilkins's life.

Mr. Ness had an occasional pupil; that is to say, he never put himself out of the way to obtain pupils, but did not refuse the entreaties sometimes made to him that he would prepare a young man for college, by allowing the said young man to reside and read with him. "Ness's men" took rather high honours, for the tutor, too indolent to find out work for himself, had a certain pride in doing well the work that was found for him.

When Ellinor was somewhere about fourteen, a young Mr. Corbet came to be pupil to Mr. Ness. Her father always called on the young men reading with the clergyman, and asked them to his house. His hospitality had in course of time lost its *recherché* and elegant character, but was always generous, and often profuse. Besides, it was in his character to like the joyous, thoughtless company of the young better than that of the old—given the same amount of refinement and education in both.

Mr. Corbet was a young man of very good family, from a distant county. If his character had not been so grave and deliberate, his years would only have entitled him to be called a boy, for he was but eighteen at the time when he came to read with Mr. Ness. But many men of five-and-twenty have not reflected so deeply as this young Mr. Corbet already had. He had considered and almost matured his plan for life; had ascertained what objects he desired most to accomplish in the dim future, which is to many at his age only a shapeless mist; and had resolved on certain steady courses of action by which such objects were most likely to be secured. A younger son, his family connections and family interest pre-arranged a legal career for him; and it was in accordance with his own tastes and talents. All, however, which his father hoped for him was, that he might be able to make an income sufficient for a gentleman to live on. Old Mr. Corbet was hardly to be called ambitious, or, if he were, his ambition was limited to views for the eldest son. But Ralph intended to be a distinguished lawyer, not so much for the vision of the woolsack, which I suppose dances before the imagination of every young lawyer, as for the grand intellectual exercise, and consequent power over mankind, that distinguished lawyers may always possess if they choose. A seat in Parliament, statesmanship, and all the great scope for a powerful and active mind that lay on each side of such a career—these were the objects which Ralph Corbet set before himself. To take high honours at college was the first step to be accomplished; and in order to achieve this Ralph had, not persuaded—persuasion was a weak instrument which he despised—but gravely reasoned his father into consenting to pay the large sum which Mr. Ness expected with a pupil. The good-natured old squire was rather pressed for ready money, but sooner than listen to an argument instead of taking his nap after dinner he would have yielded anything. But this did not satisfy Ralph; his father's reason must be convinced of the desirability of the step, as well as his weak will give way. The squire listened, looked wise, sighed; spoke of Edward's extravagance and the girls' expenses, grew sleepy, and said, "Very true," "That is but reasonable, certainly," glanced at the door, and wondered when his son would have ended his talking and go into the drawing-room; and at length found himself writing the desired letter to Mr. Ness, consenting to everything, terms and all. Mr. Ness never had a more satisfactory pupil; one whom he could treat more as an intellectual equal.

Mr. Corbet, as Ralph was always called in Hamley, was resolute in his cultivation of himself, even exceeding what his tutor demanded of him. He was greedy of information in the hours not devoted to absolute study. Mr. Ness enjoyed giving information, but most of all he liked the hard tough arguments on all metaphysical and ethical questions in which Mr. Corbet delighted to engage him. They lived together on terms of happy equality, having thus much in common. They were essentially different, however, although there were so many points of resemblance. Mr. Ness was unworldly as far as the idea of real unworldliness is compatible with a turn for self-indulgence and indolence; while Mr. Corbet was deeply, radically worldly, yet for the accomplishment of his object could deny himself all the careless pleasures natural to his age. The tutor and pupil allowed themselves one frequent relaxation, that of Mr. Wilkins's company. Mr. Ness would stroll to the office after the six hours' hard reading were over—leaving Mr. Corbet still bent over the table, book bestrewn—and see what Mr. Wilkins's engagements were. If he had nothing better to do that evening, he was either asked to dine at the parsonage, or he, in his careless hospitable way, invited the other two to dine with him, Ellinor forming the fourth at table, as far as seats went, although her dinner had been eaten early with Miss Monro. She was little and slight of her age, and her father never seemed to understand how she was passing out of childhood. Yet while in stature she was like a child; in intellect, in force of character, in strength of clinging affection, she was a woman. There might be much of the simplicity of a child about her, there was little of the undeveloped girl, varying from day to day like an April sky, careless as to which way her own character is tending. So the two young people sat with their elders, and both relished the company they were thus prematurely thrown into. Mr. Corbet talked as much as either of the other two gentlemen; opposing and disputing on any side, as if to find out how much he could urge against received opinions. Ellinor sat silent; her dark eyes flashing from time to time in vehement interest—sometimes in vehement indignation if Mr. Corbet, riding a-tilt at everyone, ventured to attack her father. He saw how this course excited her, and rather liked pursuing it in consequence; he thought it only amused him.

Another way in which Ellinor and Mr. Corbet were thrown together occasionally was this: Mr. Ness and Mr. Wilkins shared the same *Times* between them; and it was Ellinor's duty to see that the paper was regularly taken from her father's house to the parsonage. Her father liked to dawdle over it. Until Mr. Corbet had come to live with him, Mr. Ness had not much cared at what time it was passed on to him; but the young man took a strong interest in all public events, and especially in all that was said about them. He grew impatient if the paper was not forthcoming, and would set off himself to go for it, sometimes meeting the penitent breathless Ellinor in the long lane which led from Hamley to Mr. Wilkins's house. At first he used to receive her eager "Oh! I am so sorry, Mr. Corbet, but papa has only just done with it," rather gruffly. After a time he had the grace to tell her it did not signify; and by-and-by he would turn back with her to give her some advice about her garden, or her plants—for his mother and sisters were first-rate practical gardeners, and he himself was, as he expressed it, "a capital consulting physician for a sickly plant."

All this time his voice, his step, never raised the child's colour one shade the higher, never made her heart beat the least quicker, as the slightest sign of her father's approach was wont to do. She learnt to rely on Mr. Corbet for advice, for a little occasional sympathy, and for much condescending attention. He also gave her more fault-finding than all the rest of the world put together; and, curiously enough, she was grateful to him for it, for she really was humble and wished to improve. He liked the attitude of superiority which this implied and exercised right gave him. They were very good friends at present. Nothing more.

All this time I have spoken only of Mr. Wilkins's life as he stood in relation to his daughter. But there is far more to be said about it. After his wife's death, he withdrew himself from society for a year or two in a more positive and decided manner than is common with widowers. It was during this retirement of his that he riveted his little daughter's heart in such a way as to influence all her future life.

When he began to go out again, it might have been perceived—had any one cared to notice—how much the different characters of his father and wife had influenced him and kept him steady. Not that he broke out into any immoral conduct, but he gave up time to pleasure, which both old Mr. Wilkins and Lettice would have quietly induced him to spend in the office, superintending his business. His indulgence in hunting, and all field sports, had hitherto been only occasional; they now became habitual, as far as the seasons permitted. He shared a moor in Scotland with one of the Holsters one year, persuading himself that the bracing air was good for Ellinor's health. But the year afterwards he took another, this time joining with a comparative stranger; and on this moor there was no house to which it was fit to bring a child and her attendants. He persuaded himself that by frequent journeys he could make up for his absences from Hamley. But journeys cost money; and he was often away from his office when important business required attending to. There was some talk of a new attorney setting up in Hamley, to be supported by one or two of the more influential county families, who had found Wilkins not so attentive as his father. Sir Frank Holster sent for his relation, and told him of this project, speaking to him, at the same time, in pretty round terms on the folly of the life he was leading. Foolish it certainly was, and as such Mr. Wilkins was secretly acknowledging it; but when Sir Frank, lashing himself, began to talk of his hearer's presumption in joining the hunt, in aping the mode of life and amusements of the landed gentry, Edward fired up. He knew how much Sir Frank was dipped, and comparing it with the round sum his own father had left him, he said some plain truths to Sir Frank which the latter never forgave, and henceforth there was no intercourse between Holster Court and Ford Bank, as Mr. Edward Wilkins had christened his father's house on his first return from the Continent.

The conversation had two consequences besides the immediate one of the quarrel. Mr. Wilkins advertised for a responsible and confidential clerk to conduct the business under his own superintendence; and he also wrote to the Heralds' College to ask if he did not belong to the family bearing the same name in South Wales—those who have since reassumed their ancient name of De Winton.

Both applications were favorably answered. A skilful, experienced, middle-aged clerk was recommended to him by one of the principal legal firms in London, and immediately engaged to come to Hamley at his own terms; which were pretty high. But, as Mr. Wilkins said it was worth any money to pay for the relief from constant responsibility which such a business as his involved, some people remarked that he had never appeared to feel the responsibility very much hitherto, as witness his absences in Scotland, and his various social engagements when at home; it had been very different (they said) in his father's day. The Heralds' College held out hopes of affiliating him to the South Wales family, but it would require time and money to make the requisite inquiries and substantiate the claim. Now, in many a place there would be none to contest the right a man might have to assert that he belonged to such and such a family, or even to assume their arms. But it was otherwise in ---shire. Everyone was up in genealogy and heraldry, and considered filching a name and a pedigree a far worse sin than any of those mentioned on the Commandments. There were those among them who would doubt and dispute even the decision of the Heralds' College; but with it, if in his favour, Mr. Wilkins intended to be satisfied, and accordingly he wrote in reply to their letter to say, that of course he was aware such inquiries would take a considerable sum of money, but still he wished them to be made, and that speedily.

Before the end of the year he went up to London to order a brougham to be built (for Ellinor to drive out in wet weather, he said; but as going in a closed carriage always made her ill, he used it principally himself in driving to dinner-parties), with the De Winton Wilkinses' arms neatly emblazoned on panel and harness. Hitherto he had always gone about in a dog-cart—the immediate descendant of his father's old-fashioned gig.

For all this, the squires, his employers, only laughed at him and did not treat him with one whit more respect.

Mr. Dunster, the new clerk, was a quiet, respectable-looking man; you could not call him a gentleman in manner, and yet no one could say he was vulgar. He had not much varying expression on his face, but a permanent one of thoughtful consideration of the subject in hand, whatever it might be, that would have fitted as well with the profession of medicine as with that of law, and was quite the right look for either. Occasionally a bright flash of sudden intelligence lightened up his deep-sunk eyes, but even this was quickly extinguished as by some inward repression, and the habitually reflective, subdued expression returned to the face. As soon as he came into his situation, he first began quietly to arrange the papers, and next the business of which they were the outer sign, into more methodical order than they had been in since old Mr. Wilkins's death. Punctual to a moment himself, he looked his displeased surprise when the inferior clerks came tumbling in half an hour after the time in the morning; and his look was more effective than many men's words; henceforward the subordinates were within five minutes of the appointed hour for opening the office; but still he was always there before them. Mr. Wilkins himself winced under his new clerk's order and punctuality; Mr. Dunster's raised eyebrow and contraction of the lips at some woeful confusion in the business of the office, chafed Mr. Wilkins more, far more than any open expression of opinion would have done; for that he could have met, and explained away as he fancied. A secret respectful dislike grew up in his bosom against Mr. Dunster. He esteemed him, he valued him, and he could not bear him. Year after year Mr. Wilkins had become more under the influence of his feelings, and less under the command of his reason. He rather cherished than repressed his nervous repugnance to the harsh measured tones of Mr. Dunster's voice; the latter spoke with a provincial twang which grated on his employer's sensitive ear. He was annoyed at a certain green coat which his new clerk brought with him, and he watched its increasing shabbiness with a sort of childish pleasure. But by-and-by Mr. Wilkins found out that, from some perversity of taste, Mr. Dunster always had his coats, Sunday and working-day, made of this obnoxious colour; and this knowledge did not diminish his secret irritation. The worst of all, perhaps, was, that Mr. Dunster was really invaluable in many ways; "a perfect treasure," as Mr. Wilkins used to term him in speaking of him after dinner; but, for all that, he came to hate his "perfect treasure," as he gradually felt that Dunster had become so indispensable to the business that his chief could not do without him.

The clients re-echoed Mr. Wilkins's words, and spoke of Mr. Dunster as invaluable to his master; a thorough treasure, the very saving of the business. They had not been better attended to, not even in old Mr. Wilkins's days; such a clear head, such a knowledge of law, such a steady, upright fellow, always at his post. The grating voice, the drawling accent, the bottle-green coat, were nothing to them; far less noticed, in fact, than Wilkins's expensive habits, the money he paid for his wine and horses, and the nonsense of claiming kin with the Welsh Wilkinses, and setting up his brougham to drive about ---shire lanes, and be knocked to pieces over the rough round paving-stones thereof.

All these remarks did not come near Ellinor to trouble her life. To her, her dear father was the first of human beings; so sweet, so good, so kind, so charming in conversation, so full of accomplishment and information! To her healthy, happy mind every one turned their bright side. She loved Miss Monro—all the servants—especially Dixon, the coachman. He had been her father's playfellow as a boy, and, with all his respect and admiration for his master, the freedom of intercourse that had been established between them then had never been quite lost. Dixon was a fine, stalwart old fellow, and was as harmonious in his ways with his master as Mr. Dunster was discordant; accordingly he was a great favourite, and could say many a thing which might have been taken as impertinent from another servant.

He was Ellinor's great confidant about many of her little plans and projects; things that she dared not speak of to Mr. Corbet, who, after her father and Dixon, was her next best friend. This intimacy with Dixon displeased Mr. Corbet. He once or twice insinuated that he did not think it was well to talk so familiarly as Ellinor did with a servant—one out of a completely different class—such as Dixon. Ellinor did not easily take hints; every one had spoken plain out to her hitherto; so Mr. Corbet had to say his meaning plain out at last. Then, for the first time, he saw her angry; but she was too young, too childish, to have words at will to express her feelings; she only could say broken beginnings of sentences, such as "What a shame! Good, dear Dixon, who is as loyal and true and kind as any nobleman. I like him far better than you, Mr. Corbet, and I shall talk to him." And then she burst into tears and ran away, and would not come to wish Mr. Corbet good-bye, though she knew she should not see him again for a long time, as he was returning the next day to his father's house, from whence he would go to Cambridge.

He was annoyed at this result of the good advice he had thought himself bound to give to a motherless girl, who had no one to instruct her in the proprieties in which his own sisters were brought up; he left Hamley both sorry and displeased. As for Ellinor, when she found out the next day that he really was gone—gone without even coming to Ford Bank again to see if she were not penitent for her angry words—gone without saying or hearing a word of good-bye—she shut herself up in her room, and cried more bitterly than ever, because anger against herself was mixed with her regret for his loss. Luckily, her father was dining out, or he would have inquired what was the matter with his darling; and she would have had to try to explain what could not be explained. As it was, she sat with her back to the light during the schoolroom tea, and afterwards, when Miss Monro had settled down to her study of the Spanish language, Ellinor stole out into the garden, meaning to have a fresh cry over her own naughtiness and Mr. Corbet's departure; but the August evening was still and calm, and put her passionate grief to shame, hushing her up, as it were, with the other young creatures, who were being soothed to rest by the serene time of day, and the subdued light of the twilight sky.

There was a piece of ground surrounding the flower-garden, which was not shrubbery, nor wood, nor kitchen garden—only a grassy bit, out of which a group of old forest trees sprang. Their roots were heaved above ground; their leaves fell in autumn so profusely that the turf was ragged and bare in spring; but, to make up for this, there never was such a place for snowdrops.

The roots of these old trees were Ellinor's favourite play-place; this space between these two was her doll's kitchen, that its drawing-room, and so on. Mr. Corbet rather despised her contrivances for doll's furniture, so she had not often brought him here; but Dixon delighted in them, and contrived and planned with the eagerness of six years old rather than forty. To-night Ellinor went to this place, and there were all a new collection of ornaments for Miss Dolly's sitting-room made out of fir-bobs, in the prettiest and most ingenious way. She knew it was Dixon's doing and rushed off in search of him to thank him.

"What's the matter with my pretty?" asked Dixon, as soon as the pleasant excitement of thanking and being thanked was over, and he had leisure to look at her tear-stained face.

"Oh, I don't know! Never mind," said she, reddening.

Dixon was silent for a minute or two, while she tried to turn off his attention by her hurried prattle.

"There's no trouble afoot that I can mend?" asked he, in a minute or two.

"Oh, no! It's really nothing—nothing at all," said she. "It's only that Mr. Corbet went away without saying good-bye to me, that's all." And she looked as if she should have liked to cry again.

"That was not manners," said Dixon, decisively.

"But it was my fault," replied Ellinor, pleading against the condemnation.

Dixon looked at her pretty sharply from under his ragged bushy eyebrows.

"He had been giving me a lecture, and saying I didn't do what his sisters did—just as if I were to be always trying to be like somebody else—and I was cross and ran away."

"Then it was Missy who wouldn't say good-bye. That was not manners in Missy."

"But, Dixon, I don't like being lectured!"

"I reckon you don't get much of it. But, indeed, my pretty, I daresay Mr. Corbet was in the right; for, you see, master is busy, and Miss Monro is so dreadful learned, and your poor mother is dead and gone, and you have no one to teach you how young ladies go on; and by all accounts Mr. Corbet comes of a good family. I've heard say his father had the best stud-farm in all Shropshire, and spared no money upon it; and the young ladies his sisters will have been taught the best of manners; it might be well for my pretty to hear how they go on."

"You dear old Dixon, you don't know anything about my lecture, and I'm not going to tell you. Only I daresay Mr. Corbet might be a little bit right, though I'm sure he was a great deal wrong."

"But you'll not go on a-fretting—you won't now, there's a good young lady—for master won't like it, and it'll make him uneasy, and he's enough of trouble without your red eyes, bless them."

"Trouble—papa, trouble! Oh, Dixon! what do you mean?" exclaimed Ellinor, her face taking all a woman's intensity of expression in a minute.

"Nay, I know nought," said Dixon, evasively. "Only that Dunster fellow is not to my mind, and I think he potters the master sadly with his fid-fad ways."

"I hate Mr. Dunster!" said Ellinor, vehemently. "I won't speak a word to him the next time he comes to dine with papa."

"Missy will do what papa likes best," said Dixon, admonishingly; and with this the pair of "friends" parted,

CHAPTER IV.

The summer afterwards Mr. Corbet came again to read with Mr. Ness. He did not perceive any alteration in himself, and indeed his early-matured character had hardly made progress during the last twelve months whatever intellectual acquirements he might have made. Therefore it was astonishing to him to see the alteration in Ellinor Wilkins. She had shot up from a rather puny girl to a tall, slight young lady, with promise of great beauty in the face, which a year ago had only been remarkable for the fineness of the eyes. Her complexion was clear now, although colourless—twelve months ago he would have called it sallow—her delicate cheek was smooth as marble, her teeth were even and white, and her rare smiles called out a lovely dimple.

She met her former friend and lecturer with a grave shyness, for she remembered well how they had parted, and thought he could hardly have forgiven, much less forgotten, her passionate flinging away from him. But the truth was, after the first few hours of offended displeasure, he had ceased to think of it at all. She, poor child, by way of proving her repentance, had tried hard to reform her boisterous tom-boy manners, in order to show him that, although she would not give up her dear old friend Dixon, at his or anyone's bidding, she would strive to profit by his lectures in all things reasonable. The consequence was, that she suddenly appeared to him as an elegant dignified young lady, instead of the rough little girl he remembered. Still below her somewhat formal manners there lurked the old wild spirit, as he could plainly see after a little more watching; and he began to wish to call this out, and to strive, by reminding her of old days, and all her childish frolics, to flavour her subdued manners and speech with a little of the former originality.

In this he succeeded. No one, neither Mr. Wilkins, nor Miss Monro, nor Mr. Ness, saw what this young couple were about—they did not know it themselves; but before the summer was over they were desperately in love with each other, or perhaps I should rather say, Ellinor was desperately in love with him—he, as passionately as he could be with anyone; but in him the intellect was superior in strength to either affections or passions.

The causes of the blindness of those around them were these: Mr. Wilkins still considered Ellinor as a little girl, as his own pet, his darling, but nothing more. Miss Monro was anxious about her own improvement. Mr. Ness was deep in a new edition of "Horace," which he was going to bring out with notes. I believe Dixon would have been keener sighted, but Ellinor kept Mr. Corbet and Dixon apart for obvious reasons—they were each her dear friends, but she knew that Mr. Corbet did not like Dixon, and suspected that the feeling was mutual.

The only change of circumstances between this year and the previous one consisted in this development of attachment between the young people. Otherwise, everything went on apparently as usual. With Ellinor the course of the day was something like this: up early and into the garden until breakfast time, when she made tea for her father and Miss Monro in the dining-room, always taking care to lay a little nosegay of freshly-gathered flowers by her father's plate. After breakfast, when the conversation had been on general and indifferent subjects, Mr. Wilkins withdrew into the little study so often mentioned. It opened out of a passage that ran between the dining-room and the kitchen, on the left hand of the hall. Corresponding to the dining-room on the other side of the hall was the drawing-room, with its side-window serving as a door into a conservatory, and this again opened into the library. Old Mr. Wilkins had added a semicircular projection to the library, which was lighted by a dome above, and showed off his son's Italian purchases of sculpture. The library was by far the most striking and agreeable room in the house; and the consequence was that the drawing-room was seldom used, and had the aspect of cold discomfort common to apartments rarely occupied. Mr. Wilkins's study, on the other side of the house, was also an afterthought, built only a few years ago, and projecting from the regularity of the outside wall; a little stone passage led to it from the hall, small, narrow, and dark, and out of which no other door opened.

The study itself was a hexagon, one side window, one fireplace, and the remaining four sides occupied with doors, two of which have been already mentioned, another at the foot of the narrow winding stairs which led straight into Mr. Wilkins's bedroom over the dining-room, and the fourth opening into a path through the shrubbery to the right of the flower-garden as you looked from the house. This path led through the stable-yard, and then by a short cut right into Hamley, and brought you out close to Mr. Wilkins's office; it was by this way he always went and returned to his business. He used the study for a smoking and lounging room principally, although he always spoke of it as a convenient place for holding confidential communications with such of his clients as did not like discussing their business within the possible hearing of all the clerks in his office. By the outer door he could also pass to the stables, and see that proper care was taken at all times of his favourite and valuable horses. Into this study Ellinor would follow him of a morning, helping him on with his great-coat, mending his gloves, talking an infinite deal of merry fond nothing; and then, clinging to his arm, she would accompany him in his visits to the stables, going up to the shyest horses, and petting them, and patting them, and feeding them with bread all the time that her father held converse with Dixon. When he was finally gone—and sometimes it was a long time first—she returned to the schoolroom to Miss Monro, and tried to set herself hard at work on her lessons. But she had not much time for steady application; if her father had cared for her progress in anything, she would and could have worked hard at that study or accomplishment; but Mr. Wilkins, the ease and pleasure loving man, did not wish to make himself into the pedagogue, as he would have considered it, if he had ever questioned Ellinor with a real steady purpose of ascertaining her intellectual progress. It was quite enough for him that her general intelligence and variety of desultory and miscellaneous reading made her a pleasant and agreeable companion for his hours of relaxation.

At twelve o'clock, Ellinor put away her books with joyful eagerness, kissed Miss Monro, asked her if they should go a regular walk, and was always rather thankful when it was decided that it would be better to stroll in the garden—a decision very often come to, for Miss Monro hated fatigue, hated dirt, hated scrambling, and dreaded rain; all of which are evils, the chances of which are never far distant from country walks. So Ellinor danced out into the garden, worked away among her flowers, played at the old games among the roots of the trees, and, when she could, seduced Dixon into the flower-garden to have a little consultation as to the horses and dogs. For it was one of her father's few strict rules that Ellinor was never to go into the stable-yard unless he were with her; so these *tête-à-têtes* with Dixon were always held in the flower-garden, or bit of forest ground surrounding it. Miss Monro sat and basked in the sun, close to the dial, which made the centre of the gay flower-beds, upon which the dining-room and study windows looked.

At one o'clock, Ellinor and Miss Monro dined. An hour was allowed for Miss Monro's digestion, which Ellinor again spent out of doors, and at three, lessons began again and lasted till five. At that time they went to dress preparatory for the schoolroom tea at half-past five. After tea Ellinor tried to prepare her lessons for the next day; but all the time she was listening for her father's footstep—the moment she heard that, she dashed down her book, and flew out of the room to welcome and kiss him. Seven was his dinner-hour; he hardly ever dined alone; indeed, he often dined from home four days out of seven, and when he had no engagement to take him out he liked to have some one to keep him company: Mr. Ness very often, Mr. Corbet along with him if he was in Hamley, a stranger friend, or one of his clients. Sometimes, reluctantly, and when he fancied he could not avoid the attention without giving offence, Mr. Wilkins would ask Mr. Dunster, and then the two would always follow Ellinor into the library at a very early hour, as if their subjects for *tête-à-tête* conversation were quite exhausted. With all his other visitors, Mr. Wilkins sat long—yes, and yearly longer; with Mr. Ness, because they became interested in each other's conversation; with some of the others, because the wine was good, and the host hated to spare it.

Mr. Corbet used to leave his tutor and Mr. Wilkins and saunter into the library. There sat Ellinor and Miss Monro, each busy with their embroidery. He would bring a stool to Ellinor's side, question and tease her, interest her, and they would become entirely absorbed in each other, Miss Monro's sense of propriety being entirely set at rest by the consideration that Mr. Wilkins must know what he was about in allowing a young man to become thus intimate with his daughter, who, after all, was but a child.

Mr. Corbet had lately fallen into the habit of walking up to Ford Bank for *The Times* every day, near twelve o'clock, and lounging about in the garden until one; not exactly with either Ellinor or Miss Monro, but certainly far more at the beck and call of the one than of the other.

Miss Monro used to think he would have been glad to stay and lunch at their early dinner, but she never gave the invitation, and he could not well stay without her expressed sanction. He told Ellinor all about his mother and sisters, and their ways of going on, and spoke of them and of his father as of people she was one day certain to know, and to know intimately; and she did not question or doubt this view of things; she simply acquiesced.

He had some discussion with himself as to whether he should speak to her, and so secure her promise to be his before returning to Cambridge or not. He did not like the formality of an application to Mr. Wilkins, which would, after all, have been the proper and straightforward course to pursue with a girl of her age—she was barely sixteen. Not that he anticipated any difficulty on Mr. Wilkins's part; his approval of the intimacy which at their respective ages was pretty sure to lead to an attachment, was made as evident as could be by actions without words. But there would have to be reference to his own father, who had no notion of the whole affair, and would be sure to treat it as a boyish fancy; as if at twenty-one Ralph was not a man, as clear and deliberative in knowing his own mind, as resolute as he ever would be in deciding upon the course of exertion that should lead him to independence and fame, if such were to be attained by clear intellect and a strong will.

No; to Mr. Wilkins he would not speak for another year or two.

But should he tell Ellinor in direct terms of his love—his intention to marry her?

Again he inclined to the more prudent course of silence. He was not afraid of any change in his own inclinations: of them he was sure. But he looked upon it in this way: If he made a regular declaration to her she would be bound to tell it to her father. He should not respect her or like her so much if she did not. And yet this course would lead to all the conversations, and discussions, and references to his own father, which made his own direct appeal to Mr. Wilkins appear a premature step to him.

Whereas he was as sure of Ellinor's love for him as if she had uttered all the vows that women ever spoke; he knew even better than she did how fully and entirely that innocent girlish heart was his own. He was too proud to dread her inconstancy for an instant; "besides," as he went on to himself, as if to make assurance doubly sure, "whom does she see? Those stupid Holsters, who ought to be only too proud of having such a girl for their cousin, ignore her existence, and spoke slightingly of her father only the very last time I dined there. The country people in this precisely Boeotian ---shire clutch at me because my father goes up to the Plantagenets for his pedigree—not one whit for myself—and neglect Ellinor; and only condescend to her father because old Wilkins was nobody-knows-who's son. So much the worse for them, but so much the better for me in this case. I'm above their silly antiquated prejudices, and shall be only too glad when the fitting time comes to make Ellinor my wife. After all, a prosperous attorney's daughter may not be considered an unsuitable match for me—younger son as I am. Ellinor will make a glorious woman three or four years hence; just the style my father admires—such a figure, such limbs. I'll be patient, and bide my time, and watch my opportunities, and all will come right."

So he bade Ellinor farewell in a most reluctant and affectionate manner, although his words might have been spoken out in Hamley market-place, and were little different from what he said to Miss Monro. Mr. Wilkins half expected a disclosure to himself of the love which he suspected in the young man; and when that did not come, he prepared himself for a confidence from Ellinor. But she had nothing to tell him, as he very well perceived from the child's open unembarrassed manner when they were left alone together after dinner. He had refused an invitation, and shaken off Mr. Ness, in order to have this confidential *tête-à-tête* with his motherless girl; and there was nothing to make confidence of. He was half inclined to be angry; but then he saw that, although sad, she was so much at peace with herself and with the world, that he, always an optimist, began to think the young man had done wisely in not tearing open the rosebud of her feelings too prematurely.

The next two years passed over in much the same way—or a careless spectator might have thought so. I have heard people say, that if you look at a regiment advancing with steady step over a plain on a review-day, you can hardly tell that they are not merely marking time on one spot of ground, unless you compare their position with some other object by which to mark their progress, so even is the repetition of the movement. And thus the sad events of the future life of this father and daughter were hardly perceived in their steady advance, and yet over the monotony and flat uniformity of their days sorrow came marching down upon them like an armed man. Long before Mr. Wilkins had recognised its shape, it was approaching him in the distance—as, in fact, it is approaching all of us at this very time; you, reader, I, writer, have each our great sorrow bearing down upon us. It may be yet beyond the dimmest point of our horizon, but in the stillness of the night our hearts shrink at the sound of its coming footstep. Well is it for those who fall into the hands of the Lord rather than into the hands of men; but worst of all is it for him who has hereafter to mingle the gall of remorse with the cup held out to him by his doom.

Mr. Wilkins took his ease and his pleasure yet more and more every year of his life; nor did the quality of his ease and his pleasure improve; it seldom does with self-indulgent people. He cared less for any books that strained his faculties a little—less for engravings and sculptures—perhaps more for pictures. He spent extravagantly on his horses; "thought of eating and drinking." There was no open vice in all this, so that any awful temptation to crime should come down upon him, and startle him out of his mode of thinking and living; half the people about him did much the same, as far as their lives were patent to his unreflecting observation. But most of his associates had their duties to do, and did them with a heart and a will, in the hours when he was not in their company. Yes! I call them duties, though some of them might be self-imposed and purely social; they were engagements they had entered into, either tacitly or with words, and that they fulfilled. From Mr. Hetherington, the Master of the Hounds, who was up at—no one knows what hour, to go down to the kennel and see that the men did their work well and thoroughly, to stern old Sir Lionel Playfair, the upright magistrate, the thoughtful, conscientious landlord—they did their work according to their lights; there were few laggards among those with whom Mr. Wilkins associated in the field or at the dinner-table. Mr. Ness—though as a clergyman he was not so active as he might have been—yet even Mr. Ness fagged away with his pupils and his new edition of one of the classics. Only Mr. Wilkins, dissatisfied with his position, neglected to fulfil the duties thereof. He imitated the pleasures, and longed for the fancied leisure of those about him; leisure that he imagined would be so much more valuable in the hands of a man like himself, full of intellectual tastes and accomplishments, than frittered away by dull boors of untravelled, uncultivated squires—whose company, however, be it said by the way, he never refused.

And yet daily Mr. Wilkins was sinking from the intellectually to the sensually self-indulgent man. He lay late in bed, and hated Mr. Dunster for his significant glance at the office-clock when he announced to his master that such and such a client had been waiting more than an hour to keep an appointment. "Why didn't you see him yourself, Dunster? I'm sure you would have done quite as well as me," Mr. Wilkins sometimes replied, partly with a view of saying something pleasant to the man whom he disliked and feared. Mr. Dunster always replied, in a meek matter-of-fact tone, "Oh, sir, they wouldn't like to talk over their affairs with a subordinate."

And every time he said this, or some speech of the same kind, the idea came more and more clearly into Mr. Wilkins's head, of how pleasant it would be to himself to take Dunster into partnership, and thus throw all the responsibility of the real work and drudgery upon his clerk's shoulders. Importunate clients, who would make appointments at unseasonable hours and would keep to them, might confide in the partner, though they would not in the clerk. The great objections to this course were, first and foremost, Mr. Wilkins's strong dislike to Mr. Dunster—his repugnance to his company, his dress, his voice, his ways—all of which irritated his employer, till his state of feeling towards Dunster might be called antipathy; next, Mr. Wilkins was fully aware of the fact that all Mr. Dunster's actions and words were carefully and thoughtfully pre-arranged to further the great unspoken desire of his life—that of being made a partner where he now was only a servant. Mr. Wilkins took a malicious pleasure in tantalizing Mr. Dunster by such speeches as the one I have just mentioned, which always seemed like an opening to the desired end, but still for a long time never led any further. Yet all the while that end was becoming more and more certain, and at last it was reached.

Mr. Dunster always suspected that the final push was given by some circumstance from without; some reprimand for neglect—some threat of withdrawal of business which his employer had received; but of this he could not be certain; all he knew was, that Mr. Wilkins proposed the partnership to him in about as ungracious a way as such an offer could be made; an ungraciousness which, after all, had so little effect on the real matter in hand, that Mr. Dunster could pass over it with a private sneer, while taking all possible advantage of the tangible benefit it was now in his power to accept.

Mr. Corbet's attachment to Ellinor had been formally disclosed to her just before this time. He had left college, entered at the Middle Temple, and was fagging away at law, and feeling success in his own power; Ellinor was to "come out" at the next Hamley assemblies; and her lover began to be jealous of the possible admirers her striking appearance and piquant conversation might attract, and thought it a good time to make the success of his suit certain by spoken words and promises.

He needed not have alarmed himself even enough to make him take this step, if he had been capable of understanding Ellinor's heart as fully as he did her appearance and conversation. She never missed the absence of formal words and promises. She considered herself as fully engaged to him, as much pledged to marry him and no one else, before he had asked the final question, as afterwards. She was rather surprised at the necessity for those decisive words,

"Ellinor, dearest, will you—can you marry me?" and her reply was—given with a deep blush I must record, and in a soft murmuring tone—

"Yes—oh, yes—I never thought of anything else."

"Then I may speak to your father, may not I, darling?"

"He knows; I am sure he knows; and he likes you so much. Oh, how happy I am!"

"But still I must speak to him before I go. When can I see him, my Ellinor? I must go back to town at four o'clock."

"I heard his voice in the stable-yard only just before you came. Let me go and find out if he is gone to the office yet."

No! to be sure he was not gone. He was quietly smoking a cigar in his study, sitting in an easy-chair near the open window, and leisurely glancing at all the advertisements in *The Times*. He hated going to the office more and more since Dunster had become a partner; that fellow gave himself such airs of investigation and reprehension.

He got up, took the cigar out of his mouth, and placed a chair for Mr. Corbet, knowing well why he had thus formally prefaced his entrance into the room with a—

"Can I have a few minutes' conversation with you, Mr. Wilkins?"

"Certainly, my dear fellow. Sit down. Will you have a cigar?"

"No! I never smoke." Mr. Corbet despised all these kinds of indulgences, and put a little severity into his refusal, but quite unintentionally; for though he was thankful he was not as other men, he was not at all the person to trouble himself unnecessarily with their reformation.

"I want to speak to you about Ellinor. She says she thinks you must be aware of our mutual attachment."

"Well," said Mr. Wilkins—he had resumed his cigar, partly to conceal his agitation at what he knew was coming—"I believe I have had my suspicions. It is not very long since I was young myself." And he sighed over the recollection of Lettice, and his fresh, hopeful youth.

"And I hope, sir, as you have been aware of it, and have never manifested any disapprobation of it, that you will not refuse your consent—a consent I now ask you for—to our marriage."

Mr. Wilkins did not speak for a little while—a touch, a thought, a word more would have brought him to tears; for at the last he found it hard to give the consent which would part him from his only child. Suddenly he got up, and putting his hand into that of the anxious lover (for his silence had rendered Mr. Corbet anxious up to a certain point of perplexity—he could not understand the implied he would and he would not), Mr. Wilkins said,

"Yes! God bless you both! I will give her to you, some day—only it must be a long time first. And now go away—go back to her—for I can't stand this much longer."

Mr. Corbet returned to Ellinor. Mr. Wilkins sat down and buried his head in his hands, then went to his stable, and had Wildfire saddled for a good gallop over the country. Mr. Dunster waited for him in vain at the office, where an obstinate old country gentleman from a distant part of the shire would ignore Dunster's existence as a partner, and pertinaciously demanded to see Mr. Wilkins on important business.

CHAPTER V.

A few days afterwards, Ellinor's father bethought himself that same further communication ought to take place between him and his daughter's lover regarding the approval of the family of the latter to the young man's engagement, and he accordingly wrote a very gentlemanly letter, saying that of course he trusted that Ralph had informed his father of his engagement; that Mr. Corbet was well known to Mr. Wilkins by reputation, holding the position which he did in Shropshire, but that as Mr. Wilkins did not pretend to be in the same station of life, Mr. Corbet might possibly never even have heard of his name, although in his own county it was well known as having been for generations that of the principal conveyancer and land-agent of ---shire; that his wife had been a member of the old knightly family of Holsters, and that he himself was descended from a younger branch of the South Wales De Wintons, or Wilkins; that Ellinor, as his only child, would naturally inherit all his property, but that in the meantime, of course, some settlement upon her would be made, the nature of which might be decided nearer the time of the marriage.

It was a very good straightforward letter and well fitted for the purpose to which Mr. Wilkins knew it would be applied—of being forwarded to the young man's father. One would have thought that it was not an engagement so disproportionate in point of station as to cause any great opposition on that score; but, unluckily, Captain Corbet, the heir and eldest son, had just formed a similar engagement with Lady Maria Brabant, the daughter of one of the proudest earls in ---shire, who had always resented Mr. Wilkins's appearance on the field as an insult to the county, and ignored his presence at every dinner-table where they met. Lady Maria was visiting the Corbets at the very time when Ralph's letter, enclosing Mr. Wilkins's, reached the paternal halls, and she merely repeated her father's opinions when Mrs. Corbet and her daughters naturally questioned her as to who these Wilkinses were; they remembered the name in Ralph's letters formerly; the father was some friend of Mr. Ness's, the clergyman with whom Ralph had read; they believed Ralph used to dine with these Wilkinses sometimes, along with Mr. Ness.

Lady Maria was a goodnatured girl, and meant no harm in repeating her father's words; touched up, it is true, by some of the dislike she herself felt to the intimate alliance proposed, which would make her sister-in-law to the daughter of an "upstart attorney," "not received in the county," "always trying to push his way into the set above him," "claiming connection with the De Wintons of --- Castle, who, as she well knew, only laughed when he was spoken of, and said they were more rich in relations than they were aware of"—"not people papa would ever like her to know, whatever might be the family connection."

These little speeches told in a way which the girl who uttered them did not intend they should. Mrs. Corbet and her daughters set themselves violently against this foolish entanglement of Ralph's; they would not call it an engagement. They argued, and they urged, and they pleaded, till the squire, anxious for peace at any price, and always more under the sway of the people who were with him, however unreasonable they might be, than of the absent, even though these had the wisdom of Solomon or the prudence and sagacity of his son Ralph, wrote an angry letter, saying that, as Ralph was of age, of course he had a right to please himself, therefore all his father could say was, that the engagement was not at all what either he or Ralph's mother had expected or hoped; that it was a degradation to the family just going to ally themselves with a peer of James the First's creation; that of course Ralph must do what he liked, but that if he married this girl he must never expect to have her received by the Corbets of Corbet Hall as a daughter. The squire was rather satisfied with his production, and took it to show it to his wife; but she did not think it was strong enough, and added a little postscript

"DEAR RALPH,

"Though, as second son, you are entitled to Bromley at my death, yet I can do much to make the estate worthless. Hitherto, regard for you has prevented my taking steps as to sale of timber, &c., which would materially increase your sisters' portions; this just measure I shall infallibly take if I find you persevere in keeping to this silly engagement. Your father's disapproval is always a sufficient reason to allege."

Ralph was annoyed at the receipt of these letters, though he only smiled as he locked them up in his desk.

"Dear old father! how he blusters! As to my mother, she is reasonable when I talk to her. Once give her a definite idea of what Ellinor's fortune will be, and let her, if she chooses, cut down her timber—a threat she has held over me ever since I knew what a rocking-horse was, and which I have known to be illegal these ten years past—and she'll come round. I know better than they do how Reginald has run up post-obits, and as for that vulgar high-born Lady Maria they are all so full of, why, she is a Flanders mare to my Ellinor, and has not a silver penny to cross herself with, besides! I bide my time, you dear good people!"

He did not think it necessary to reply to these letters immediately, nor did he even allude to their contents in his to Ellinor. Mr. Wilkins, who had been very well satisfied with his own letter to the young man, and had thought that it must be equally agreeable to every one, was not at all suspicious of any disapproval, because the fact of a distinct sanction on the part of Mr. Ralph Corbet's friends to his engagement was not communicated to him.

As for Ellinor, she trembled all over with happiness. Such a summer for the blossoming of flowers and ripening of fruit had not been known for years; it seemed to her as if bountiful loving Nature wanted to fill the cup of Ellinor's joy to overflowing, and as if everything, animate and inanimate, sympathised with her happiness. Her father was well, and apparently content. Miss Monro was very kind. Dixon's lameness was quite gone off. Only Mr. Dunster came creeping about the house, on pretence of business, seeking out her father, and disturbing all his leisure with his dust-coloured parchment-skinned careworn face, and seeming to disturb the smooth current of her daily life whenever she saw him.

Ellinor made her appearance at the Hamley assemblies, but with less *éclat* than either her father or her lover expected. Her beauty and natural grace were admired by those who could discriminate; but to the greater number there was (what they called) "a want of style"—want of elegance there certainly was not, for her figure was perfect, and though she moved shyly, she moved well. Perhaps it was not a good place for a correct appreciation of Miss Wilkins; some of the old dowagers thought it a piece of presumption in her to be there at all—but the Lady Holster of the day (who remembered her husband's quarrel with Mr. Wilkins, and looked away whenever Ellinor came near) resented this opinion. "Miss Wilkins is descended from Sir Frank's family, one of the oldest in the county; the objection might have been made years ago to the father, but as he had been received, she did not know why Miss Wilkins was to be alluded to as out of her place." Ellinor's greatest enjoyment in the evening was to hear her father say, after all was over, and they were driving home—

"Well, I thought my Nelly the prettiest girl there, and I think I know some other people who would have said the same if they could have spoken out."

"Thank you, papa," said Ellinor, squeezing his hand, which she held. She thought he alluded to the absent Ralph as the person who would have agreed with him, had he had the opportunity of seeing her; but no, he seldom thought much of the absent; but had been rather flattered by seeing Lord Hildebrand take up his glass for the apparent purpose of watching Ellinor.

"Your pearls, too, were as handsome as any in the room, child—but we must have them re-set; the sprays are old-fashioned now. Let me have them to-morrow to send up to Hancock."

"Papa, please, I had rather keep them as they are—as mamma wore them."

He was touched in a minute.

"Very well, darling. God bless you for thinking of it!"

But he ordered her a set of sapphires instead, for the next assembly.

These balls were not such as to intoxicate Ellinor with success, and make her in love with gaiety. Large parties came from the different country-houses in the neighbourhood, and danced with each other. When they had exhausted the resources they brought with them, they had generally a few dances to spare for friends of the same standing with whom they were most intimate. Ellinor came with her father, and joined an old card-playing dowager, by way of a chaperone—the said dowager being under old business obligations to the firm of Wilkins and Son, and apologizing to all her acquaintances for her own weak condescension to Mr. Wilkins's foible in wishing to introduce his daughter into society above her natural sphere. It was upon this lady, after she had uttered some such speech as the one I have just mentioned, that Lady Holster had come down with the pedigree of Ellinor's mother. But though the old dowager had drawn back a little discomfited at my lady's reply, she was not more attentive to Ellinor in consequence. She allowed Mr. Wilkins to bring in his daughter and place her on the crimson sofa beside her; spoke to her occasionally in the interval that elapsed before the rubbers could be properly arranged in the card-room; invited the girl to accompany her to that sober amusement, and on Ellinor's declining, and preferring to remain with her father, the dowager left her with a sweet smile on her plump countenance, and an approving conscience somewhere within her portly frame, assuring her that she had done all that could possibly have been expected from her towards "that good Wilkins's daughter." Ellinor stood by her father watching the dances, and thankful for the occasional chance of a dance. While she had been sitting by her chaperone, Mr. Wilkins had made the tour of the room, dropping out the little fact of his daughter's being present wherever he thought the seed likely to bring forth the fruit of partners. And some came because they liked Mr. Wilkins, and some asked Ellinor because they had done their duty dances to their own party, and might please themselves. So that she usually had an average of one invitation to every three dances; and this principally towards the end of the evening.

But considering her real beauty, and the care which her father always took about her appearance, she met with far less than her due of admiration. Admiration she did not care for; partners she did; and sometimes felt mortified when she had to sit or stand quiet during all the first part of the evening. If it had not been for her father's wishes she would much rather have stayed at home; but, nevertheless, she talked even to the irresponsive old dowager, and fairly chatted to her father when she got beside him, because she did not like him to fancy that she was not enjoying herself.

And, indeed, she had so much happiness in the daily course of this part of her life, that, on looking back upon it afterwards, she could not imagine anything brighter than it had been. The delight of receiving her lover's letters—the anxious happiness of replying to them (always a little bit fearful lest she should not express herself and her love in the precisely happy medium becoming a maiden)—the father's love and satisfaction in her—the calm prosperity of the whole household—was delightful at the time, and, looking back upon it, it was dreamlike.

Occasionally Mr. Corbet came down to see her. He always slept on these occasions at Mr. Ness's; but he was at Ford Bank the greater part of the one day between two nights that he allowed himself for the length of his visits. And even these short peeps were not frequently taken. He was working hard at law: fagging at it tooth and nail; arranging his whole life so as best to promote the ends of his ambition; feeling a delight in surpassing and mastering his fellows—those who started in the race at the same time. He read Ellinor's letters over and over again; nothing else beside law-books. He perceived the repressed love hidden away in subdued expressions in her communications, with an amused pleasure at the attempt at concealment. He was glad that her gaieties were not more gay; he was glad that she was not too much admired, although a little indignant at the want of taste on the part of the ---shire gentlemen. But if other admirers had come prominently forward, he would have had to take some more decided steps to assert his rights than he had hitherto done; for he had caused Ellinor to express a wish to her father that her engagement should not be too much talked about until nearer the time when it would be prudent for him to marry her. He thought that the knowledge of this, the only imprudently hasty step he ever meant to take in his life, might go against his character for wisdom, if the fact became known while he was as yet only a student. Mr. Wilkins wondered a little; but acceded, as he always did, to any of Ellinor's requests. Mr. Ness was a confidant, of course, and some of Lady Maria's connections heard of it, and forgot it again very soon; and, as it happened, no one else was sufficiently interested in Ellinor to care to ascertain the fact.

All this time, Mr. Ralph Corbet maintained a very quietly decided attitude towards his own family. He was engaged to Miss Wilkins; and all he could say was, he felt sorry that they disapproved of it. He was not able to marry just at present, and before the time for his marriage arrived, he trusted that his family would take a more reasonable view of things, and be willing to receive her as his wife with all becoming respect or affection. This was the substance of what he repeated in different forms in reply to his father's angry letters. At length, his invariable determination made way with his father; the paternal thunderings were subdued to a distant rumbling in the sky; and presently the inquiry was broached as to how much fortune Miss Wilkins would have; how much down on her marriage; what were the eventual probabilities. Now this was a point which Mr. Ralph Corbet himself wished to be informed upon. He had not thought much about it in making the engagement; he had been too young, or too much in love. But an only child of a wealthy attorney ought to have something considerable; and an allowance so as to enable the young couple to start housekeeping in a moderately good part of town, would be an advantage to him in his profession. So he replied to his father, adroitly suggesting that a letter containing certain modifications of the inquiry which had been rather roughly put in Mr. Corbet's last, should be sent to him, in order that he might himself ascertain from Mr. Wilkins what were Ellinor's prospects as regarded fortune.

The desired letter came; but not in such a form that he could pass it on to Mr. Wilkins; he preferred to make quotations, and even these quotations were a little altered and dressed before he sent them on. The gist of his letter to Mr. Wilkins was this. He stated that he hoped soon to be in a position to offer Ellinor a home; that he anticipated a steady progress in his profession, and consequently in his income; but that contingencies might arise, as his father suggested, which would deprive him of the power of earning a livelihood, perhaps when it might be more required than it would be at first; that it was true that, after his mother's death a small estate in Shropshire would come to him as second son, and of course Ellinor would receive the benefit of this property, secured to her legally as Mr. Wilkins thought best—that being a matter for after discussion—but that at present his father was anxious, as might be seen from the extract to ascertain whether Mr. Wilkins could secure him from the contingency of having his son's widow and possible children thrown upon his hands, by giving Ellinor a dowry; and if so, it was gently insinuated, what would be the amount of the same.

When Mr. Wilkins received this letter it startled him out of a happy day-dream. He liked Ralph Corbet and the whole connection quite well enough to give his consent to an engagement; and sometimes even he was glad to think that Ellinor's future was assured, and that she would have a protector and friends after he was dead and gone. But he did not want them to assume their responsibilities so soon. He had not distinctly contemplated her marriage as an event likely to happen before his death. He could not understand how his own life would go on without her: or indeed why she and Ralph Corbet could not continue just as they were at present. He came down to breakfast with the letter in his hand. By Ellinor's blushes, as she glanced at the handwriting, he knew that she had heard from her lover by the same post; by her tender caresses—caresses given as if to make up for the pain which the prospect of her leaving him was sure to cause him—he was certain that she was aware of the contents of the letter. Yet he put it in his pocket, and tried to forget it.

He did this not merely from his reluctance to complete any arrangements which might facilitate Ellinor's marriage. There was a further annoyance connected with the affair. His money matters had been for some time in an involved state; he had been living beyond his income, even reckoning that, as he always did, at the highest point which it ever touched. He kept no regular accounts, reasoning with himself—or, perhaps, I should rather say persuading himself—that there was no great occasion for regular accounts, when he had a steady income arising from his profession, as well as the interest of a good sum of money left him by his father; and when, living in his own house near a country town where provisions were cheap, his expenditure for his small family—only one child—could never amount to anything like his incomings from the above-mentioned sources. But servants and horses, and choice wines and rare fruit-trees, and a habit of purchasing any book or engraving that may take the fancy, irrespective of the price, run away with money, even though there be but one child. A year or two ago, Mr. Wilkins had been startled into a system of exaggerated retrenchment—retrenchment which only lasted about six weeks—by the sudden bursting of a bubble speculation in which he had invested a part of his father's savings. But as soon as the change in his habits, necessitated by his new economies, became irksome, he had comforted himself for his relapse into his former easy extravagance of living by remembering the fact that Ellinor was engaged to the son of a man of large property: and that though Ralph was only the second son, yet his mother's estate must come to him, as Mr. Ness had already mentioned, on first hearing of her engagement.

Mr. Wilkins did not doubt that he could easily make Ellinor a fitting allowance, or even pay down a requisite dowry; but the doing so would involve an examination into the real state of his affairs, and this involved distasteful trouble. He had no idea how much more than mere temporary annoyance would arise out of the investigation. Until it was made, he decided in his own mind that he would not speak to Ellinor on the subject of her lover's letter. So for the next few days she was kept in suspense, seeing little of her father; and during the short times she was with him she was made aware that he was nervously anxious to keep the conversation engaged on general topics rather than on the one which she had at heart. As I have already said, Mr. Corbet had written to her by the same post as that on which he sent the letter to her father, telling her of its contents, and begging her (in all those sweet words which lovers know how to use) to urge her father to compliance for his sake—his, her lover's—who was pining and lonely in all the crowds of London, since her loved presence was not there. He did not care for money, save as a means of hastening their marriage; indeed, if there were only some income fixed, however small—some time for their marriage fixed, however distant—he could be patient. He did not want superfluity of wealth; his habits were simple, as she well knew; and money enough would be theirs in time, both from her share of contingencies, and the certainty of his finally possessing Bromley.

Ellinor delayed replying to this letter until her father should have spoken to her on the subject. But as she perceived that he avoided all such conversation, the young girl's heart failed her. She began to blame herself for wishing to leave him, to reproach herself for being accessory to any step which made him shun being alone with her, and look distressed and full of care as he did now. It was the usual struggle between father and lover for the possession of love, instead of the natural and graceful resignation of the parent to the prescribed course of things; and, as usual, it was the poor girl who bore the suffering for no fault of her own: although she blamed herself for being the cause of the disturbance in the previous order of affairs. Ellinor had no one to speak to confidentially but her father and her lover, and when they were at issue she could talk openly to neither, so she brooded over Mr. Corbet's unanswered letter, and her father's silence, and became pale and dispirited. Once or twice she looked up suddenly, and caught her father's eye gazing upon her with a certain wistful anxiety; but the instant she saw this he pulled himself up, as it were, and would begin talking gaily about the small topics of the day.

At length Mr. Corbet grew impatient at not hearing either from Mr. Wilkins or Ellinor, and wrote urgently to the former, making known to him a new proposal suggested to him by his father, which was, that a certain sum should be paid down by Mr. Wilkins to be applied, under the management of trustees, to the improvement of the Bromley estate, out of the profits of which, or other sources in the elder Mr. Corbet's hands, a heavy rate of interest should be paid on this advance, which would secure an income to the young couple immediately, and considerably increase the value of the estate upon which Ellinor's settlement was to be made. The terms offered for this laying down of ready money were so advantageous, that Mr. Wilkins was strongly tempted to accede to them at once; as Ellinor's pale cheek and want of appetite had only that very morning smote upon his conscience, and this immediate transfer of ready money was as a sacrifice, a soothing balm to his self-reproach, and laziness and dislike to immediate unpleasantness of action had its counterbalancing weakness in imprudence. Mr. Wilkins made some rough calculations on a piece of paper—deeds, and all such tests of accuracy, being down at the office; discovered that he could pay down the sum required; wrote a letter agreeing to the proposal, and before he sealed it called Ellinor into his study, and bade her read what he had been writing and tell him what she thought of it. He watched the colour come rushing into her white face, her lips quiver and tremble, and even before the letter was ended she was in his arms kissing him, and thanking him with blushing caresses rather than words.

"There, there!" said he, smiling and sighing; "that will do. Why, I do believe you took me for a hard-hearted father, just like a heroine's father in a book. You've looked as woe-begone this week past as Ophelia. One can't make up one's mind in a day about such sums of money as this, little woman; and you should have let your old father have time to consider."

"Oh, papa; I was only afraid you were angry."

"Well, if I was a bit perplexed, seeing you look so ill and pining was not the way to bring me round. Old Corbet, I must say, is trying to make a good bargain for his son. It is well for me that I have never been an extravagant man."

"But, papa, we don't want all this much."

"Yes, yes! it is all right. You shall go into their family as a well-portioned girl, if you can't go as a Lady Maria. Come, don't trouble your little head any more about it. Give me one more kiss, and then we'll go and order the horses, and have a ride together, by way of keeping holiday. I deserve a holiday, don't I, Nelly?"

Some country people at work at the roadside, as the father and daughter passed along, stopped to admire their bright happy looks, and one spoke of the hereditary handsomeness of the Wilkins family (for the old man, the present Mr. Wilkins's father, had been fine-looking in his drab breeches and gaiters, and usual assumption of a yeoman's dress). Another said it was easy for the rich to be handsome; they had always plenty to eat, and could ride when they were tired of walking, and had no care for the morrow to keep them from sleeping at nights. And, in sad acquiescence with their contrasted lot, the men went on with their hedging and ditching in silence.

And yet, if they had known—if the poor did know—the troubles and temptations of the rich; if those men had foreseen the lot darkening over the father, and including the daughter in its cloud; if Mr. Wilkins himself had even imagined such a future possible . . . Well, there was truth in the old heathen saying, "Let no man be envied till his death."

Ellinor had no more rides with her father; no, not ever again; though they had stopped that afternoon at the summit of a breezy common, and looked at a ruined hall, not so very far off; and discussed whether they could reach it that day, and decided that it was too far away for anything but a hurried inspection, and that some day soon they would make the old place into the principal object of an excursion. But a rainy time came on, when no rides were possible; and whether it was the influence of the weather, or some other care or trouble that oppressed him, Mr. Wilkins seemed to lose all wish for much active exercise, and rather sought a stimulus to his spirits and circulation in wine. But of this Ellinor was innocently unaware. He seemed dull and weary, and sat long, drowsing and drinking after dinner. If the servants had not been so fond of him for much previous generosity and kindness, they would have complained now, and with reason, of his irritability, for all sorts of things seemed to annoy him.

"You should get the master to take a ride with you, miss," said Dixon, one day as he was putting Ellinor on her horse. "He's not looking well, he's studying too much at the office."

But when Ellinor named it to her father, he rather hastily replied that it was all very well for women to ride out whenever they liked—men had something else to do; and then, as he saw her look grave and puzzled, he softened down his abrupt saying by adding that Dunster had been making a fuss about his partner's non-attendance, and altogether taking a good deal upon himself in a very offensive way, so that he thought it better to go pretty regularly to the office, in order to show him who was master—senior partner, and head of the business, at any rate.

Ellinor sighed a little over her disappointment at her father's preoccupation, and then forgot her own little regret in anger at Mr. Dunster, who had seemed all along to be a thorn in her father's side, and had latterly gained some power and authority over him, the exercise of which, Ellinor could not help thinking, was a very impertinent line of conduct from a junior partner, so lately only a paid clerk, to his superior. There was a sense of something wrong in the Ford Bank household for many weeks about this time. Mr. Wilkins was not like himself, and his cheerful ways and careless genial speeches were missed, even on the days when he was not irritable, and evidently uneasy with himself and all about him. The spring was late in coming, and cold rain and sleet made any kind of out-door exercise a trouble and discomfort rather than a bright natural event in the course of the day. All sound of winter gaieties, of assemblies and meets, and jovial dinners, had died away, and the summer pleasures were as yet unthought of. Still Ellinor had a secret perennial source of sunshine in her heart; whenever she thought of Ralph she could not feel much oppression from the present unspoken and indistinct gloom. He loved her; and oh, how she loved him! and perhaps this very next autumn—but that depended on his own success in his profession. After all, if it was not this autumn it would be the next; and with the letters that she received weekly, and the occasional visits that her lover ran down to Hamley to pay Mr. Ness, Ellinor felt as if she would almost prefer the delay of the time when she must leave her father's for a husband's roof.

CHAPTER VI.

At Easter—just when the heavens and earth were looking their dreariest, for Easter fell very early this year—Mr. Corbet came down. Mr. Wilkins was too busy to see much of him; they were together even less than usual, although not less friendly when they did meet. But to Ellinor the visit was one of unmixed happiness. Hitherto she had always had a little fear mingled up with her love of Mr. Corbet; but his manners were softened, his opinions less decided and abrupt, and his whole treatment of her showed such tenderness, that the young girl basked and revelled in it. One or two of their conversations had reference to their future married life in London; and she then perceived, although it did not jar against her, that her lover had not forgotten his ambition in his love. He tried to inoculate her with something of his own craving for success in life; but it was all in vain: she nestled to him, and told him she did not care to be the Lord Chancellor's wife—wigs and wool-sacks were not in her line; only if he wished it, she would wish it.

The last two days of his stay the weather changed. Sudden heat burst forth, as it does occasionally for a few hours even in our chilly English spring. The grey-brown bushes and trees started almost with visible progress into the tender green shade which is the forerunner of the bursting leaves. The sky was of full cloudless blue. Mr. Wilkins was to come home pretty early from the office to ride out with his daughter and her lover; but, after waiting some time for him, it grew too late, and they were obliged to give up the project. Nothing would serve Ellinor, then, but that she must carry out a table and have tea in the garden, on the sunny side of the tree, among the roots of which she used to play when a child. Miss Monro objected a little to this caprice of Ellinor's, saying that it was too early for out-of-door meals; but Mr. Corbet overruled all objections, and helped her in her gay preparations. She always kept to the early hours of her childhood, although she, as then, regularly sat with her father at his late dinner; and this meal *al fresco* was to be a reality to her and Miss Monro. There was a place arranged for her father, and she seized upon him as he was coming from the stable-yard, by the shrubbery path, to his study, and with merry playfulness made him a prisoner, accusing him of disappointing them of their ride, and drawing him more than half unwilling, to his chair by the table. But he was silent, and almost sad: his presence damped them all; they could hardly tell why, for he did not object to anything, though he seemed to enjoy nothing, and only to force a smile at Ellinor's occasional sallies. These became more and more rare as she perceived her father's depression. She watched him anxiously. He perceived it, and said—shivering in that strange unaccountable manner which is popularly explained by the expression that some one is passing over the earth that will one day form your grave—"Ellinor! this is not a day for out-of-door tea. I never felt so chilly a spot in my life. I cannot keep from shaking where I sit. I must leave this place, my dear, in spite of all your good tea."

"Oh, papa! I am so sorry. But look how full that hot sun's rays come on this turf. I thought I had chosen such a capital spot!"

But he got up and persisted in leaving the table, although he was evidently sorry to spoil the little party. He walked up and down the gravel walk, close by them, talking to them as he kept passing by and trying to cheer them up.

"Are you warmer now, papa?" asked Ellinor.

"Oh, yes! All right. It's only that place that seems so chilly and damp. I'm as warm as a toast now."

The next morning Mr. Corbet left them. The unseasonably fine weather passed away too, and all things went back to their rather grey and dreary aspect; but Ellinor was too happy to feel this much, knowing what absent love existed for her alone, and from this knowledge unconsciously trusting in the sun behind the clouds.

I have said that few or none in the immediate neighbourhood of Hamley, beside their own household and Mr. Ness, knew of Ellinor's engagement. At one of the rare dinner-parties to which she accompanied her father—it was at the old lady's house who chaperoned her to the assemblies—she was taken in to dinner by a young clergyman staying in the neighbourhood. He had just had a small living given to him in his own county, and he felt as if this was a great step in his life. He was good, innocent, and rather boyish in appearance. Ellinor was happy and at her ease, and chatted away to this Mr. Livingstone on many little points of interest which they found they had in common: church music, and the difficulty they had in getting people to sing in parts; Salisbury Cathedral, which they had both seen; styles of church architecture, Ruskin's works, and parish schools, in which Mr. Livingstone was somewhat shocked to find that Ellinor took no great interest. When the gentleman came in from the dining-room, it struck Ellinor, for the first time in her life, that her father had taken more wine than was good for him. Indeed, this had rather become a habit with him of late; but as he always tried to go quietly off to his own room when such had been the case, his daughter had never been aware of it before, and the perception of it now made her cheeks hot with shame. She thought that everyone must be as conscious of his altered manner and way of speaking as she was, and after a pause of sick silence, during which she could not say a word, she set to and talked to Mr. Livingstone about parish schools, anything, with redoubled vigour and apparent interest, in order to keep one or two of the company, at least, from noticing what was to her so painfully obvious.

The effect of her behaviour was far more than she had intended. She kept Mr. Livingstone, it is true, from observing her father, but she also riveted his attention on herself. He had thought her very pretty and agreeable during dinner: but after dinner he considered her bewitching, irresistible. He dreamed of her all night, and wakened up the next morning to a calculation of how far his income would allow him to furnish his pretty new parsonage with that crowning blessing, a wife. For a day or two he did up little sums, and sighed, and thought of Ellinor, her face listening with admiring interest to his sermons, her arm passed into his as they went together round the parish; her sweet voice instructing classes in his schools—turn where he would, in his imagination Ellinor's presence rose up before him.

The consequence was that he wrote an offer, which he found a far more perplexing piece of composition than a sermon; a real hearty expression of love, going on, over all obstacles, to a straightforward explanation of his present prospects and future hopes, and winding up with the information that on the succeeding morning he would call to know whether he might speak to Mr. Wilkins on the subject of this letter. It was given to Ellinor in the evening, as she was sitting with Miss Monro in the library. Mr. Wilkins was dining out, she hardly knew where, as it was a sudden engagement, of which he had sent word from the office—a gentleman's dinner-party, she supposed, as he had dressed in Hamley without coming home. Ellinor turned over the letter when it was brought to her, as some people do when they cannot recognise the handwriting, as if to discover from paper or seal what two moments would assure them of, if they opened the letter and looked at the signature. Ellinor could not guess who had written it by any outward sign; but the moment she saw the name "Herbert Livingstone," the meaning of the letter flashed upon her and she coloured all over. She put the letter away, unread, for a few minutes, and then made some excuse for leaving the room and going upstairs. When safe in her bed-chamber, she read the young man's eager words with a sense of self-reproach. How must she, engaged to one man, have been behaving to another, if this was the result of a single evening's interview? The self-reproach was unjustly bestowed; but with that we have nothing to do. She made herself very miserable; and at last went down with a heavy heart to go on with Dante, and rummage up words in the dictionary. All the time she seemed to Miss Monro to be plodding on with her Italian more diligently and sedately than usual, she was planning in her own mind to speak to her father as soon as he returned (and he had said that he should not be late), and beg him to undo the mischief she had done by seeing Mr. Livingstone the next morning, and frankly explaining the real state of affairs to him. But she wanted to read her letter again, and think it all over in peace; and so, at an early hour, she wished Miss Monro good-night, and went up into her own room above the drawing-room, and overlooking the flower-garden and shrubbery-path to the stable-yard, by which her father was sure to return. She went upstairs and studied her letter well, and tried to recall all her speeches and conduct on that miserable evening—as she thought it then—not knowing what true misery was. Her head ached, and she put out the candle, and went and sat on the window-seat, looking out into the moonlit garden, watching for her father. She opened the window; partly to cool her forehead, partly to enable her to call down softly when she should see him coming along. By-and-by the door from the stable-yard into the shrubbery clicked and opened, and in a moment she saw Mr. Wilkins moving through the bushes; but not alone, Mr. Dunster was with him, and the two were talking together in rather excited tones, immediately lost to hearing, however, as they entered Mr. Wilkins's study by the outer door.

"They have been dining together somewhere. Probably at Mr. Hanbury's" (the Hamley brewer), thought Ellinor. "But how provoking that he should have come home with papa this night of all nights!"

Two or three times before Mr. Dunster had called on Mr. Wilkins in the evening, as Ellinor knew; but she was not quite aware of the reason for such late visits, and had never put together the two facts—(as cause and consequence)—that on such occasions her father had been absent from the office all day, and that there might be necessary business for him to transact, the urgency of which was the motive for Mr. Dunster's visits. Mr. Wilkins always seemed to be annoyed by his coming at so late an hour, and spoke of it, resenting the intrusion upon his leisure; and Ellinor, without consideration, adopted her father's mode of speaking and thinking on the subject, and was rather more angry than he was whenever the obnoxious partner came on business in the evening. This night was, of all nights, the most ill-purposed time (so Ellinor thought) for a *tête-à-tête* with her father! However, there was no doubt in her mind as to what she had to do. So late as it was, the unwelcome visitor could not stop long; and then she would go down and have her little confidence with her father, and beg him to see Mr. Livingstone when he came next morning, and dismiss him as gently as might be.

She sat on in the window-seat; dreaming waking dreams of future happiness. She kept losing herself in such thoughts, and became almost afraid of forgetting why she sat there. Presently she felt cold, and got up to fetch a shawl, in which she muffled herself and resumed her place. It seemed to her growing very late; the moonlight was coming fuller and fuller into the garden and the blackness of the shadow was more concentrated and stronger. Surely Mr. Dunster could not have gone away along the dark shrubbery-path so noiselessly but what she must have heard him? No! there was the swell of voices coming up through the window from her father's study: angry voices they were; and her anger rose sympathetically, as she knew that her father was being irritated. There was a sudden movement, as of chairs pushed hastily aside, and then a mysterious unaccountable noise—heavy, sudden; and then a slight movement as of chairs again; and then a profound stillness. Ellinor leaned her head against the side of the window to listen more intently, for some mysterious instinct made her sick and faint. No sound—no noise. Only by-and-by she heard, what we have all heard at such times of intent listening, the beating of the pulses of her heart, and then the whirling rush of blood through her head. How long did this last? She never knew. By-and-by she heard her father's hurried footstep in his bedroom, next to hers; but when she ran thither to speak to him, and ask him what was amiss—if anything had been—if she might come to him now about Mr. Livingstone's letter, she found that he had gone down again to his study, and almost at the same moment she heard the little private outer door of that room open; some one went out, and then there were hurried footsteps along the shrubbery-path. She thought, of course, that it was Mr. Dunster leaving the house; and went back for Mr. Livingstone's letter. Having found it, she passed through her father's room to the private staircase, thinking that if she went by the more regular way, she would have run the risk of disturbing Miss Monro, and perhaps of being questioned in the morning. Even in passing down this remote staircase, she trod softly for fear of being overheard. When she entered the room, the full light of the candles dazzled her for an instant, coming out of the darkness. They were flaring wildly in the draught that came in through the open door, by which the outer air was admitted; for a moment there seemed no one in the room, and then she saw, with strange sick horror, the legs of some one lying on the carpet behind the table. As if compelled, even while she shrank from doing it, she went round to see who it was that lay there, so still and motionless as never to stir at her sudden coming. It was Mr. Dunster; his head propped on chair-cushions, his eyes open, staring, distended. There was a strong smell of brandy and hartshorn in the room; a smell so powerful as not to be neutralized by the free current of night air that blew through the two open doors. Ellinor could not have told whether it was reason or instinct that made her act as she did during this awful night. In thinking of it afterwards, with shuddering avoidance of the haunting memory that would come and overshadow her during many, many years of her life, she grew to believe that the powerful smell of the spilt brandy absolutely intoxicated her—an unconscious Rechabite in practice. But something gave her a presence of mind and a courage not her own. And though she learnt to think afterwards that she had acted unwisely, if not wrongly and wickedly, yet she marvelled, in recalling that time, how she could have then behaved as she did. First of all she lifted herself up from her fascinated gaze at the dead man, and went to the staircase door, by which she had entered the study, and shut it softly. Then she went back—looked again; took the brandy-bottle, and knelt down, and tried to pour some into the mouth; but this she found she could not do. Then she wetted her handkerchief with the spirit, and moistened the lips; all to no purpose; for, as I have said before, the man was dead—killed by rupture of a vessel of the brain; how occasioned I must tell by-and-by. Of course, all Ellinor's little cares and efforts produced no effect; her father had tried them before—vain endeavours all, to bring back the precious breath of life! The poor girl could not bear the look of those open eyes, and softly, tenderly, tried to close them, although unconscious that in so doing she was rendering the pious offices of some beloved hand to a dead man. She was sitting by the body on the floor when she heard steps coming with rushing and yet cautious tread, through the shrubbery; she had no fear, although it might be the tread of robbers and murderers. The awfulness of the hour raised her above common fears; though she did not go through the usual process of reasoning, and by it feel assured that the feet which were coming so softly and swiftly along were the same which she had heard leaving the room in like manner only a quarter of an hour before.

Her father entered, and started back, almost upsetting some one behind him by his recoil, on seeing his daughter in her motionless attitude by the dead man.

"My God, Ellinor! what has brought you here?" he said, almost fiercely.

But she answered as one stupefied, "I don't know. Is he dead?"

"Hush, hush, child; it cannot be helped."

She raised her eyes to the solemn, pitying, awe-stricken face behind her father's—the countenance of Dixon.

"Is he dead?" she asked of him.

The man stepped forwards, respectfully pushing his master on one side as he did so. He bent down over the corpse, and looked, and listened and then reaching a candle off the table, he signed Mr. Wilkins to close the door. And Mr. Wilkins obeyed, and looked with an intensity of eagerness almost amounting to faintness on the experiment, and yet he could not hope. The flame was steady—steady and pitilessly unstirred, even when it was adjusted close to mouth and nostril; the head was raised up by one of Dixon's stalwart arms, while he held the candle in the other hand. Ellinor fancied that there was some trembling on Dixon's part, and grasped his wrist tightly in order to give it the requisite motionless firmness.

All in vain. The head was placed again on the cushions, the servant rose and stood by his master, looked sadly on the dead man, whom, living, none of them had liked or cared for, and Ellinor sat on, quiet and tearless, as one in a trance.

"How was it, father?" at length she asked.

He would fain have had her ignorant of all, but so questioned by her lips, so adjured by her eyes in the very presence of death, he could not choose but speak the truth; he spoke it in convulsive gasps, each sentence an effort:

"He taunted me—he was insolent, beyond my patience—I could not bear it. I struck him—I can't tell how it was. He must have hit his head in falling. Oh, my God! one little hour a go I was innocent of this man's blood!" He covered his face with his hands.

Ellinor took the candle again; kneeling behind Mr. Dunster's head, she tried the futile experiment once more.

"Could not a doctor do some good?" she asked of Dixon, in a hopeless voice.

"No!" said he, shaking his head, and looking with a sidelong glance at his master, who seemed to shrivel up and to shrink away at the bare suggestion. "Doctors can do nought, I'm afeard. All that a doctor could do, I take it, would be to open a vein, and that I could do along with the best of them, if I had but my fleam here." He fumbled in his pockets as he spoke, and, as chance would it, the "fleam" (or cattle lancet) was somewhere about his dress. He drew it out, smoothed and tried it on his finger. Ellinor tried to bare the arm, but turned sick as she did so. Her father started eagerly forwards, and did what was necessary with hurried trembling hands. If they had cared less about the result, they might have been more afraid of the consequences of the operation in the hands of one so ignorant as Dixon. But, vein or artery, it signified little; no living blood gushed out; only a little watery moisture followed the cut of the fleam. They laid him back on his strange sad death-couch. Dixon spoke next.

"Master Ned!" said he—for he had known Mr. Wilkins in his days of bright careless boyhood, and almost was carried back to them by the sense of charge and protection which the servant's presence of mind and sharpened senses gave him over his master on this dreary night—"Master Ned! we must do summut."

No one spoke. What was to be done?

"Did any folk see him come here?" Dixon asked, after a time. Ellinor looked up to hear her father's answer, a wild hope coming into her mind that all might be concealed somehow; she did not know how, nor did she think of any consequences except saving her father from the vague dread, trouble, and punishment that she was aware would await him if all were known.

Mr. Wilkins did not seem to hear; in fact, he did not hear anything but the unspoken echo of his own last words, that went booming through his heart: "An hour ago I was innocent of this man's blood! Only an hour ago!"

Dixon got up and poured out half a tumblerful of raw spirit from the brandy-bottle that stood on the table.

"Drink this, Master Ned!" putting it to his master's lips. "Nay"—to Ellinor—"it will do him no harm; only bring back his senses, which, poor gentleman, are scared away. We shall need all our wits. Now, sir, please answer my question. Did anyone see Measter Dunster come here?"

"I don't know," said Mr. Wilkins, recovering his speech. "It all seems in a mist. He offered to walk home with me; I did not want him. I was almost rude to him to keep him off. I did not want to talk of business; I had taken too much wine to be very clear and some things at the office were not quite in order, and he had found it out. If anyone heard our conversation, they must know I did not want him to come with me. Oh! why would he come? He was as obstinate—he would come—and here it has been his death!"

"Well, sir, what's done can't be undone, and I'm sure we'd any of us bring him back to life if we could, even by cutting off our hands, though he was a mighty plaguey chap while he'd breath in him. But what I'm thinking is this: it'll maybe go awkward with you, sir, if he's found here. One can't say. But don't you think, miss, as he's neither kith nor kin to miss him, we might just bury him away before morning, somewhere? There's better nor four hours of dark. I wish we could put him i' the churchyard, but that can't be; but, to my mind, the sooner we set about digging a place for him to lie in, poor fellow, the better it'll be for us all in the end. I can pare a piece of turf up where it'll never be missed, and if master'll take one spade, and I another, why we'll lay him softly down, and cover him up, and no one'll be the wiser."

There was no reply from either for a minute or so. Then Mr. Wilkins said:

"If my father could have known of my living to this! Why, they will try me as a criminal; and you, Ellinor? Dixon, you are right. We must conceal it, or I must cut my throat, for I never could live through it. One minute of passion, and my life blasted!"

"Come along, sir," said Dixon; "there's no time to lose." And they went out in search of tools; Ellinor following them, shivering all over, but begging that she might be with them, and not have to remain in the study with—

She would not be bidden into her own room; she dreaded inaction and solitude. She made herself busy with carrying heavy baskets of turf, and straining her strength to the utmost; fetching all that was wanted, with soft swift steps.

Once, as she passed near the open study door, she thought that she heard a rustling, and a flash of hope came across her. Could he be reviving? She entered, but a moment was enough to undeceive her; it had only been a night rustle among the trees. Of hope, life, there was none.

They dug the hole deep and well; working with fierce energy to quench thought and remorse. Once or twice her father asked for brandy, which Ellinor, reassured by the apparently good effect of the first dose, brought to him without a word; and once at her father's suggestion she brought food, such as she could find in the dining-room without disturbing the household, for Dixon.

When all was ready for the reception of the body in its unblessed grave, Mr. Wilkins bade Ellinor go up to her own room—she had done all she could to help them; the rest must be done by them alone. She felt that it must; and indeed both her nerves and her bodily strength were giving way. She would have kissed her father, as he sat wearily at the head of the grave—Dixon had gone in to make some arrangement for carrying the corpse—but he pushed her away quietly, but resolutely—

"No, Nelly, you must never kiss me again; I am a murderer."

"But I will, my own darling papa," said she, throwing her arms passionately round his neck, and covering his face with kisses. "I love you, and I don't care what you are, if you were twenty times a murderer, which you are not; I am sure it was only an accident."

"Go in, my child, go in, and try to get some rest. But go in, for we must finish as fast as we can. The moon is down; it will soon be daylight. What a blessing there are no rooms on one side of the house. Go, Nelly." And she went; straining herself up to move noiselessly, with eyes averted, through the room which she shuddered at as the place of hasty and unhallowed death.

Once in her own room she bolted the door on the inside, and then stole to the window, as if some fascination impelled her to watch all the proceedings to the end. But her aching eyes could hardly penetrate through the thick darkness, which, at the time of the year of which I am speaking, so closely precedes the dawn. She could discern the tops of the trees against the sky, and could single out the well-known one, at a little distance from the stem of which the grave was made, in the very piece of turf over which so lately she and Ralph had had their merry little tea-making; and where her father, as she now remembered, had shuddered and shivered, as if the ground on which his seat had then been placed was fateful and ominous to him.

Those below moved softly and quietly in all they did; but every sound had a significant and terrible interpretation to Ellinor's ears. Before they had ended, the little birds had begun to pipe out their gay *reveillée* to the dawn. Then doors closed, and all was profoundly still.

Ellinor threw herself, in her clothes, on the bed; and was thankful for the intense weary physical pain which took off something of the anguish of thought—anguish that she fancied from time to time was leading to insanity.

By-and-by the morning cold made her instinctively creep between the blankets; and, once there, she fell into a dead heavy sleep.

CHAPTER VII.

Ellinor was awakened by a rapping at her door: it was her maid.

She was fully aroused in a moment, for she had fallen asleep with one clearly defined plan in her mind, only one, for all thoughts and cares having no relation to the terrible event were as though they had never been. All her purpose was to shield her father from suspicion. And to do this she must control herself—heart, mind, and body must be ruled to this one end.

So she said to Mason:

"Let me lie half an hour longer; and beg Miss Monro not to wait breakfast for me; but in half an hour bring me up a cup of strong tea, for I have a bad headache."

Mason went away. Ellinor sprang up; rapidly undressed herself, and got into bed again, so that when her maid returned with her breakfast, there was no appearance of the night having been passed in any unusual manner.

"How ill you do look, miss!" said Mason. "I am sure you had better not get up yet."

Ellinor longed to ask if her father had yet shown himself; but this question—so natural at any other time—seemed to her so suspicious under the circumstances, that she could not bring her lips to frame it. At any rate, she must get up and struggle to make the day like all other days. So she rose, confessing that she did not feel very well, but trying to make light of it, and when she could think of anything but the one awe, to say a trivial sentence or two. But she could not recollect how she behaved in general, for her life hitherto had been simple, and led without any consciousness of effect.

Before she was dressed, a message came up to say that Mr. Livingstone was in the drawing-room.

Mr. Livingstone! He belonged to the old life of yesterday! The billows of the night had swept over his mark on the sands of her memory; and it was only by a strong effort that she could remember who he was—what he wanted. She sent Mason down to inquire from the servant who admitted him whom it was that he had asked for.

"He asked for master first. But master has not rung for his water yet, so James told him he was not up. Then he took thought for a while, and asked could he speak to you, he would wait if you were not at liberty but that he wished particular to see either master, or you. So James asked him to sit down in the drawing-room, and he would let you know."

"I must go," thought Ellinor. "I will send him away directly; to come, thinking of marriage to a house like this—to-day, too!"

And she went down hastily, and in a hard unsparing mood towards a man, whose affection for her she thought was like a gourd, grown up in a night, and of no account, but as a piece of foolish, boyish excitement.

She never thought of her own appearance—she had dressed without looking in the glass. Her only object was to dismiss her would-be suitor as speedily as possible. All feelings of shyness, awkwardness, or maiden modesty, were quenched and overcome. In she went.

He was standing by the mantelpiece as she entered. He made a step or two forward to meet her; and then stopped, petrified, as it were, at the sight of her hard white face.

"Miss Wilkins, I am afraid you are ill! I have come too early. But I have to leave Hamley in half an hour, and I thought—Oh, Miss Wilkins! what have I done?"

For she sank into the chair nearest to her, as if overcome by his words; but, indeed, it was by the oppression of her own thoughts: she was hardly conscious of his presence.

He came a step or two nearer, as if he longed to take her in his arms and comfort and shelter her; but she stiffened herself and arose, and by an effort walked towards the fireplace, and there stood, as if awaiting what he would say next. But he was overwhelmed by her aspect of illness. He almost forgot his own wishes, his own suit, in his desire to relieve her from the pain, physical as he believed it, under which she was suffering. It was she who had to begin the subject.

"I received your letter yesterday, Mr. Livingstone. I was anxious to see you to-day, in order that I might prevent you from speaking to my father. I do not say anything of the kind of affection you can feel for me—me, whom you have only seen once. All I shall say is, that the sooner we both forget what I must call folly, the better."

She took the airs of a woman considerably older and more experienced than himself. He thought her haughty; she was only miserable.

"You are mistaken," said he, more quietly and with more dignity than was likely from his previous conduct. "I will not allow you to characterise as folly what might be presumptuous on my part—I had no business to express myself so soon—but which in its foundation was true and sincere. That I can answer for most solemnly. It is possible, though it may not be a usual thing, for a man to feel so strongly attracted by the charms and qualities of a woman, even at first sight, as to feel sure that she, and she alone, can make his happiness. My folly consisted—there you are right—in even dreaming that you could return my feelings in the slightest degree, when you had only seen me once: and I am most truly ashamed of myself. I cannot tell you how sorry I am, when I see how you have compelled yourself to come and speak to me when you are so ill."

She staggered into a chair, for with all her wish for his speedy dismissal, she was obliged to be seated. His hand was upon the bell.

"No, don't!" she said. "Wait a minute."

His eyes, bent upon her with a look of deep anxiety, touched her at that moment, and she was on the point of shedding tears; but she checked herself, and rose again.

"I will go," said he. "It is the kindest thing I can do. Only, may I write? May I venture to write and urge what I have to say more coherently?"

"No!" said she. "Don't write. I have given you my answer. We are nothing, and can be nothing to each other. I am engaged to be married. I should not have told you if you had not been so kind. Thank you. But go now."

The poor young man's face fell, and he became almost as white as she was for the instant. After a moment's reflection, he took her hand in his, and said:

"May God bless you, and him too, whoever he be! But if you want a friend, I may be that friend, may I not? and try to prove that my words of regard were true, in a better and higher sense than I used them at first." And kissing her passive hand, he was gone and she was left sitting alone.

But solitude was not what she could bear. She went quickly upstairs, and took a strong dose of sal-volatile, even while she heard Miss Monro calling to her.

"My dear, who was that gentleman that has been closeted with you in the drawing-room all this time?"

And then, without listening to Ellinor's reply, she went on:

"Mrs. Jackson has been here" (it was at Mrs. Jackson's house that Mr. Dunster lodged), "wanting to know if we could tell her where Mr. Dunster was, for he never came home last night at all. And you were in the drawing-room with—who did you say he was?—that Mr. Livingstone, who might have come at a better time to bid good-bye; and he had never dined here, had he? so I don't see any reason he had to come calling, and P. P. C.-ing, and your papa *not* up. So I said to Mrs. Jackson, 'I'll send and ask Mr. Wilkins, if you like, but I don't see any use in it, for I can tell you just as well as anybody, that Mr. Dunster is not in this house, wherever he may be.' Yet nothing would satisfy her but that some one must go and waken up your papa, and ask if he could tell where Mr. Dunster was."

"And did papa?" inquired Ellinor, her dry throat huskily forming the inquiry that seemed to be expected from her.

"No! to be sure not. How should Mr. Wilkins know? As I said to Mrs. Jackson, 'Mr. Wilkins is not likely to know where Mr. Dunster spends his time when he is not in the office, for they do not move in the same rank of life, my good woman; and Mrs. Jackson apologised, but said that yesterday they had both been dining at Mr. Hodgson's together, she believed; and somehow she had got it into her head that Mr. Dunster might have missed his way in coming along Moor Lane, and might have slipped into the canal; so she just thought she would step up and ask Mr. Wilkins if they had left Mr. Hodgson's together, or if your papa had driven home. I asked her why she had not told me all these particulars before, for I could have asked your papa myself all about when he last saw Mr. Dunster; and I went up to ask him a second time, but he did not like it at all, for he was busy dressing, and I had to shout my questions through the door, and he could not always hear me at first."

"What did he say?"

"Oh! he had walked part of the way with Mr. Dunster, and then cut across by the short path through the fields, as far as I could understand him through the door. He seemed very much annoyed to hear that Mr. Dunster had not been at home all night; but he said I was to tell Mrs. Jackson that he would go to the office as soon as he had had his breakfast, which he ordered to be sent up directly into his own room, and he had no doubt it would all turn out right, but that she had better go home at once. And, as I told her, she might find Mr. Dunster there by the time she got there. There, there is your papa going out! He has not lost any time over his breakfast!"

Ellinor had taken up the *Hamley Examiner*, a daily paper, which lay on the table, to hide her face in the first instance; but it served a second purpose, as she glanced languidly over the columns of the advertisements.

"Oh! here are Colonel Macdonald's orchideous plants to be sold. All the stock of hothouse and stove plants at Hartwell Priory. I must send James over to Hartwell to attend the sale. It is to last for three days."

"But can he be spared for so long?"

"Oh, yes; he had better stay at the little inn there, to be on the spot. Three days," and as she spoke, she ran out to the gardener, who was sweeping up the newly-mown grass in the front of the house. She gave him hasty and unlimited directions, only seeming intent—if any one had been suspiciously watching her words and actions—to hurry him off to the distant village, where the auction was to take place.

When he was once gone she breathed more freely. Now, no one but the three cognisant of the terrible reason of the disturbance of the turf under the trees in a certain spot in the belt round the flower-garden, would be likely to go into the place. Miss Monro might wander round with a book in her hand; but she never noticed anything, and was short-sighted into the bargain. Three days of this moist, warm, growing weather, and the green grass would spring, just as if life—was what it had been twenty-four hours before.

When all this was done and said, it seemed as if Ellinor's strength and spirit sank down at once. Her voice became feeble, her aspect wan; and although she told Miss Monro that nothing was the matter, yet it was impossible for any one who loved her not to perceive that she was far from well. The kind governess placed her pupil on the sofa, covered her feet up warmly, darkened the room, and then stole out on tiptoe, fancying that Ellinor would sleep. Her eyes were, indeed, shut; but try as much as she would to be quiet, she was up in less than five minutes after Miss Monro had left the room, and walking up and down in all the restless agony of body that arises from an overstrained mind. But soon Miss Monro reappeared, bringing with her a dose of soothing medicine of her own concocting, for she was great in domestic quackery. What the medicine was Ellinor did not care to know; she drank it without any sign of her usual merry resistance to physic of Miss Monro's ordering; and as the latter took up a book, and showed a set purpose of remaining with her patient, Ellinor was compelled to lie still, and presently fell asleep.

She awakened late in the afternoon with a start. Her father was standing over her, listening to Miss Monro's account of her indisposition. She only caught one glimpse of his strangely altered countenance, and hid her head in the cushions—hid it from memory, not from him. For in an instant she must have conjectured the interpretation he was likely to put upon her shrinking action, and she had turned towards him, and had thrown her arms round his neck, and was kissing his cold, passive face. Then she fell back. But all this time their sad eyes never met—they dreaded the look of recollection that must be in each other's gaze.

"There, my dear!" said Miss Monro. "Now you must lie still till I fetch you a little broth. You are better now, are not you?"

"You need not go for the broth, Miss Monro," said Mr. Wilkins, ringing the bell. "Fletcher can surely bring it." He dreaded the being left alone with his daughter—nor did she fear it less. She heard the strange alteration in her father's voice, hard and hoarse, as if it was an effort to speak. The physical signs of his suffering cut her to the heart; and yet she wondered how it was that they could both be alive, or, if alive, they were not rending their garments and crying aloud. Mr. Wilkins seemed to have lost the power of careless action and speech, it is true. He wished to leave the room now his anxiety about his daughter was relieved, but hardly knew how to set about it. He was obliged to think about the veriest trifle, in order that by an effort of reason he might understand how he should have spoken or acted if he had been free from blood-guiltiness. Ellinor understood all by intuition. But henceforward the unspoken comprehension of each other's hidden motions made their mutual presence a burdensome anxiety to each. Miss Monro was a relief; they were glad of her as a third person, unconscious of the secret which constrained them. This afternoon her unconsciousness gave present pain, although on after reflection each found in her speeches a cause of rejoicing.

"And Mr. Dunster, Mr. Wilkins, has he come home yet?"

A moment's pause, in which Mr. Wilkins pumped the words out of his husky throat:

"I have not heard. I have been riding. I went on business to Mr. Estcourt's. Perhaps you will be so kind as to send and inquire at Mrs. Jackson's."

Ellinor sickened at the words. She had been all her life a truthful plain-spoken girl. She held herself high above deceit. Yet, here came the necessity for deceit—a snare spread around her. She had not revolted so much from the deed which brought unpremeditated death, as she did from these words of her father's. The night before, in her mad fever of affright, she had fancied that to conceal the body was all that would be required; she had not looked forward to the long, weary course of small lies, to be done and said, involved in that one mistaken action. Yet, while her father's words made her soul revolt, his appearance melted her heart, as she caught it, half turned away from her, neither looking straight at Miss Monro, nor at anything materially visible. His hollow sunken eye seemed to Ellinor to have a vision of the dead man before it. His cheek was livid and worn, and its healthy colouring gained by years of hearty out-door exercise, was all gone into the wanness of age. His hair, even to Ellinor, seemed greyer for the past night of wretchedness. He stooped, and looked dreamily earthward, where formerly he had stood erect. It needed all the pity called forth by such observation to quench Ellinor's passionate contempt for the course on which she and her father were embarked, when she heard him repeat his words to the servant who came with her broth.

"Fletcher! go to Mrs. Jackson's and inquire if Mr. Dunster is come home yet. I want to speak to him."

"To him!" lying dead where he had been laid; killed by the man who now asked for his presence. Ellinor shut her eyes, and lay back in despair. She wished she might die, and be out of this horrible tangle of events.

Two minutes after, she was conscious of her father and Miss Monro stealing softly out of the room. They thought that she slept.

She sprang off the sofa and knelt down.

"Oh, God," she prayed, "Thou knowest! Help me! There is none other help but Thee!"

I suppose she fainted. For, an hour or more afterwards Miss Monro, coming in, found her lying insensible by the side of the sofa.

She was carried to bed. She was not delirious, she was only in a stupor, which they feared might end in delirium. To obviate this, her father sent far and wide for skilful physicians, who tended her, almost at the rate of a guinea the minute.

People said how hard it was upon Mr. Wilkins, that scarcely had that wretch Dunster gone off, with no one knows how much out of the trusts of the firm, before his only child fell ill. And, to tell the truth, he himself looked burnt and scared with affliction. He had a startled look, they said, as if he never could tell, after such experience, from which side the awful proofs of the uncertainty of earth would appear, the terrible phantoms of unforeseen dread. Both rich and poor, town and country, sympathised with him. The rich cared not to press their claims, or their business, at such a time; and only wondered, in their superficial talk after dinner, how such a good fellow as Wilkins could ever have been deceived by a man like Dunster. Even Sir Frank Holster and his lady forgot their old quarrel, and came to inquire after Ellinor, and sent her hothouse fruit by the bushel.

Mr. Corbet behaved as an anxious lover should do. He wrote daily to Miss Monro to beg for the most minute bulletins; he procured everything in town that any doctor even fancied might be of service, he came down as soon as there was the slightest hint of permission that Ellinor might see him. He overpowered her with tender words and caresses, till at last she shrank away from them, as from something too bewildering, and past all right comprehension.

But one night before this, when all windows and doors stood open to admit the least breath that stirred the sultry July air, a servant on velvet tiptoe had stolen up to Ellinor's open door, and had beckoned out of the chamber of the sleeper the ever watchful nurse, Miss Monro.

"A gentleman wants you," were all the words the housemaid dared to say so close to the bedroom. And softly, softly Miss Monro stepped down the stairs, into the drawing-room; and there she saw Mr. Livingstone. But she did not know him;

she had never seen him before.

"I have travelled all day. I heard she was ill—was dying. May I just have one more look at her? I will not speak; I will hardly breathe. Only let me see her once again!"

"I beg your pardon, sir, but I don't know who you are; and if you mean Miss Wilkins, by 'her,' she is very ill, but we hope not dying. She was very ill, indeed, yesterday; very dangerously ill, I may say, but she is having a good sleep, in consequence of a soporific medicine, and we are really beginning to hope—"

But just here Miss Monro's hand was taken, and, to her infinite surprise, was kissed before she could remember how improper such behaviour was.

"God bless you, madam, for saying so. But if she sleeps, will you let me see her? it can do no harm, for I will tread as if on egg shells; and I have come so far—if I might just look on her sweet face. Pray, madam, let me just have one sight of her. I will not ask for more."

But he did ask for more after he had had his wish. He stole upstairs after Miss Monro, who looked round reproachfully at him if even a nightingale sang, or an owl hooted in the trees outside the open windows, yet who paused to say herself, outside Mr. Wilkins's chamber door,

"Her father's room; he has not been in bed for six nights, till to-night; pray do not make a noise to waken him." And on into the deep stillness of the hushed room, where one clear ray of hidden lamp-light shot athwart the door, where a watcher, breathing softly, sat beside the bed—where Ellinor's dark head lay motionless on the white pillow, her face almost as white, her form almost as still. You might have heard a pin fall. After a while he moved to withdraw. Miss Monro, jealous of every sound, followed him, with steps all the more heavy because they were taken with so much care, down the stairs, back into the drawing-room. By the bed-candle flaring in the draught, she saw that there was the glittering mark of wet tears on his cheek; and she felt, as she said afterwards, "sorry for the young man." And yet she urged him to go, for she knew that she might be wanted upstairs. He took her hand, and wrung it hard.

"Thank you. She looked so changed—oh! she looked as though she were dead. You will write—Herbert Livingstone, Langham Vicarage, Yorkshire; you will promise me to write. If I could do anything for her, but I can but pray. Oh, my darling; my darling! and I have no right to be with her."

"Go away, there's a good young man," said Miss Monro, all the more pressing to hurry him out by the front door, because she was afraid of his emotion overmastering him, and making him noisy in his demonstrations. "Yes, I will write; I will write, never fear!" and she bolted the door behind him, and was thankful.

Two minutes afterwards there was a low tap; she undid the fastenings, and there he stood, pale in the moonlight.

"Please don't tell her I came to ask about her; she might not like it."

"No, no! not I! Poor creature, she's not likely to care to hear anything this long while. She never roused at Mr. Corbet's name."

"Mr. Corbet's!" said Livingstone, below his breath, and he turned and went away; this time for good.

But Ellinor recovered. She knew she was recovering, when day after day she felt involuntary strength and appetite return. Her body seemed stronger than her will; for that would have induced her to creep into her grave, and shut her eyes for ever on this world, so full of troubles.

She lay, for the most part, with her eyes closed, very still and quiet; but she thought with the intensity of one who seeks for lost peace, and cannot find it. She began to see that if in the mad impulses of that mad nightmare of horror, they had all strengthened each other, and dared to be frank and open, confessing a great fault, a greater disaster, a greater woe—which in the first instance was hardly a crime—their future course, though sad and sorrowful, would have been a simple and straightforward one to tread. But it was not for her to undo what was done, and to reveal the error and shame of a father. Only she, turning anew to God, in the solemn and quiet watches of the night, made a covenant, that in her conduct, her own personal individual life, she would act loyally and truthfully. And as for the future, and all the terrible chances involved in it, she would leave it in His hands—if, indeed (and here came in the Tempter), He would watch over one whose life hereafter must seem based upon a lie. Her only plea, offered "standing afar off" was, "The lie is said and done and over—it was not for my own sake. Can filial piety be so overcome by the rights of justice and truth, as to demand of me that I should reveal my father's guilt."

Her father's severe sharp punishment began. He knew why she suffered, what made her young strength falter and tremble, what made her life seem nigh about to be quenched in death. Yet he could not take his sorrow and care in the natural manner. He was obliged to think how every word and deed would be construed. He fancied that people were watching him with suspicious eyes, when nothing was further from their thoughts. For once let the "public" of any place be possessed by an idea, it is more difficult to dislodge it than any one imagines who has not tried. If Mr. Wilkins had gone into Hamley market-place, and proclaimed himself guilty of the manslaughter of Mr. Dunster—nay, if he had detailed all the circumstances—the people would have exclaimed, "Poor man, he is crazed by this discovery of the unworthiness of the man he trusted so; and no wonder—it was such a thing to have done—to have defrauded his partner to such an extent, and then have made off to America!"

For many small circumstances, which I do not stop to detail here, went far to prove this, as we know, unfounded supposition; and Mr. Wilkins, who was known, from his handsome boyhood, through his comely manhood, up to the present time, by all the people in Hamley, was an object of sympathy and respect to every one who saw him, as he passed by, old, and lorn, and haggard before his time, all through the evil conduct of one, London-bred, who was as a hard, unlovely stranger to the popular mind of this little country town.

Mr. Wilkins's own servants liked him. The workings of his temptations were such as they could understand. If he had been hot-tempered he had also been generous, or I should rather say careless and lavish with his money. And now that he was cheated and impoverished by his partner's delinquency, they thought it no wonder that he drank long and deep in the solitary evenings which he passed at home. It was not that he was without invitations. Every one came forward to testify their respect for him by asking him to their houses. He had probably never been so universally popular since his father's death. But, as he said, he did not care to go into society while his daughter was so ill—he had no spirits for company.

But if any one had cared to observe his conduct at home, and to draw conclusions from it, they could have noticed that, anxious as he was about Ellinor, he rather avoided than sought her presence, now that her consciousness and memory were restored. Nor did she ask for, or wish for him. The presence of each was a burden to the other. Oh, sad and woeful night of May—overshadowing the coming summer months with gloom and bitter remorse!

CHAPTER VIII.

Still youth prevailed over all. Ellinor got well, as I have said, even when she would fain have died. And the afternoon came when she left her room. Miss Monro would gladly have made a festival of her recovery, and have had her conveyed into the unused drawing-room. But Ellinor begged that she might be taken into the library—into the schoolroom—anywhere (thought she) not looking on the side of the house on the flower-garden, which she had felt in all her illness as a ghastly pressure lying within sight of those very windows, through which the morning sun streamed right upon her bed—like the accusing angel, bringing all hidden things to light.

And when Ellinor was better still, when the Bath-chair had been sent up for her use, by some kindly old maid, out of Hamley, she still petitioned that it might be kept on the lawn or town side of the house, away from the flower-garden.

One day she almost screamed, when, as she was going to the front door, she saw Dixon standing ready to draw her, instead of Fletcher the servant who usually went. But she checked all demonstration of feeling; although it was the first time she had seen him since he and she and one more had worked their hearts out in hard bodily labour.

He looked so stern and ill! Cross, too, which she had never seen him before.

As soon as they were out of immediate sight of the windows, she asked him to stop, forcing herself to speak to him.

"Dixon, you look very poorly," she said, trembling as she spoke.

"Ay!" said he. "We didn't think much of it at the time, did we, Miss Nelly? But it'll be the death on us, I'm thinking. It has aged me above a bit. All my fifty years afore were but as a forenoon of child's play to that night. Measter, too—I could a-bear a good deal, but measter cuts through the stable-yard, and past me, wi'out a word, as if I was poison, or a stinking foumart. It's that as is worst, Miss Nelly, it is."

And the poor man brushed some tears from his eyes with the back of his withered, furrowed hand. Ellinor caught the infection, and cried outright, sobbed like a child, even while she held out her little white thin hand to his grasp. For as soon as he saw her emotion, he was penitent for what he had said.

"Don't now—don't," was all he could think of to say.

"Dixon!" said she at length, "you must not mind it. You must try not to mind it. I see he does not like to be reminded of that, even by seeing me. He tries never to be alone with me. My poor old Dixon, it has spoilt my life for me; for I don't think he loves me any more."

She sobbed as if her heart would break; and now it was Dixon's turn to be comforter.

"Ah, dear, my blessing, he loves you above everything. It's only he can't a-bear the sight of us, as is but natural. And if he doesn't fancy being alone with you, there's always one as does, and that's a comfort at the worst of times. And don't ye fret about what I said a minute ago. I were put out because measter all but pushed me out of his way this morning, without never a word. But I were an old fool for telling ye. And I've really forgotten why I told Fletcher I'd drag ye a bit about to-day. Th' gardener is beginning for to wonder as you don't want to see th' annuals and bedding-out things as you were so particular about in May. And I thought I'd just have a word wi' ye, and then if you'd let me, we'd go together just once round the flower-garden, just to say you've been, you know, and to give them chaps a bit of praise. You'll only have to look on the beds, my pretty, and it must be done some time. So come along!"

He began to pull resolutely in the direction of the flower-garden. Ellinor bit her lips to keep in the cry of repugnance that rose to them. As Dixon stopped to unlock the door, he said:

"It's not hardness, nothing like it; I've waited till I heerd you were better; but it's in for a penny in for a pound wi' us all; and folk may talk; and bless your little brave heart, you'll stand a deal for your father's sake, and so will I, though I do feel it above a bit, when he puts out his hand as if to keep me off, and I only going to speak to him about Clipper's knees; though I'll own I had wondered many a day when I was to have the good-morrow master never missed sin' he were a boy till—Well! and now you've seen the beds, and can say they looked mighty pretty, and is done all as you wished; and we're got out again, and breathing fresher air than yon sunbaked hole, with its smelling flowers, not half so wholesome to snuff at as good stable-dung."

So the good man chatted on; not without the purpose of giving Ellinor time to recover herself; and partly also to drown his own cares, which lay heavier on his heart than he could say. But he thought himself rewarded by Ellinor's thanks, and warm pressure of his hard hand as she got out at the front door, and bade him good-by.

The break to her days of weary monotony was the letters she constantly received from Mr. Corbet. And yet here again lurked the sting. He was all astonishment and indignation at Mr. Dunster's disappearance, or rather flight, to America. And now that she was growing stronger, he did not scruple to express curiosity respecting the details, never doubting but that she was perfectly acquainted with much that he wanted to know; although he had too much delicacy to question her on the point which was most important of all in his eyes, namely, how far it had affected Mr. Wilkins's worldly prospects; for the report prevalent in Hamley had reached London, that Mr. Dunster had made away with, or carried off, trust property to a considerable extent, for all which Mr. Wilkins would of course be liable.

It was hard work for Ralph Corbet to keep from seeking direct information on this head from Mr. Ness, or, indeed, from Mr. Wilkins himself. But he restrained himself, knowing that in August he should be able to make all these inquiries personally. Before the end of the long vacation he had hoped to marry Ellinor: that was the time which had been planned by them when they had met in the early spring before her illness and all this misfortune happened. But now, as he wrote to his father, nothing could be definitely arranged until he had paid his visit to Hamley, and seen the state of affairs.

Accordingly one Saturday in August, he came to Ford Bank, this time as a visitor to Ellinor's home, instead of to his old quarters at Mr. Ness's.

The house was still as if asleep in the full heat of the afternoon sun, as Mr. Corbet drove up. The window-blinds were down; the front door wide open, great stands of heliotrope and roses and geraniums stood just within the shadow of the hall; but through all the silence his approach seemed to excite no commotion. He thought it strange that he had not been watched for, that Ellinor did not come running out to meet him, that she allowed Fletcher to come and attend to his luggage, and usher him into the library just like any common visitor, any morning-caller. He stiffened himself up into a moment's indignant coldness of manner. But it vanished in an instant when, on the door being opened, he saw Ellinor standing holding by the table, looking for his appearance with almost panting anxiety. He thought of nothing then but her evident weakness, her changed looks, for which no account of her illness had prepared him. For she was deadly white, lips and all; and her dark eyes seemed unnaturally enlarged, while the caves in which they were set were strangely deep and hollow. Her hair, too, had been cut off pretty closely; she did not usually wear a cap, but with some faint idea of making herself look better in his eye, she had put on one this day, and the effect was that she seemed to be forty years of age; but one instant after he had come in, her pale face was flooded with crimson, and her eyes were full of tears. She had hard work to keep herself from going into hysterics, but she instinctively knew how much he would hate a scene, and she checked herself in time.

"Oh," she murmured, "I am so glad to see you; it is such a comfort, such an infinite pleasure." And so she went on, cooing out words over him, and stroking his hair with her thin fingers; while he rather tried to avert his eyes, he was so much afraid of betraying how much he thought her altered.

But when she came down, dressed for dinner, this sense of her change was diminished to him. Her short brown hair had already a little wave, and was ornamented by some black lace; she wore a large black lace shawl—it had been her mother's of old—over some delicate-coloured muslin dress; her face was slightly flushed, and had the tints of a wild rose; her lips kept pale and trembling with involuntary motion, it is true; and as the lovers stood together, hand in hand, by the window, he was aware of a little convulsive twitching at every noise, even while she seemed gazing in tranquil pleasure on the long smooth slope of the newly-mown lawn, stretching down to the little brook that prattled merrily over the stones on its merry course to Hamley town.

He felt a stronger twitch than ever before; even while his ear, less delicate than hers, could distinguish no peculiar sound. About two minutes after Mr. Wilkins entered the room. He came up to Mr. Corbet with a warm welcome: some of it real, some of it assumed. He talked volubly to him, taking little or no notice of Ellinor, who dropped into the background, and sat down on the sofa by Miss Monro; for on this day they were all to dine together. Ralph Corbet thought that Mr. Wilkins was aged; but no wonder, after all his anxiety of various kinds: Mr. Dunster's flight and reported defalcations, Ellinor's illness, of the seriousness of which her lover was now convinced by her appearance.

He would fain have spoken more to her during the dinner that ensued, but Mr. Wilkins absorbed all his attention, talking and questioning on subjects that left the ladies out of the conversation almost perpetually. Mr. Corbet recognised his host's fine tact, even while his persistence in talking annoyed him. He was quite sure that Mr. Wilkins was anxious to spare his daughter any exertion beyond that—to which, indeed, she seemed scarely equal—of sitting at the head of the table. And the more her father talked—so fine an observer was Mr. Corbet—the more silent and depressed Ellinor appeared. But by-and-by he accounted for this inverse ratio of gaiety, as he perceived how quickly Mr. Wilkins had his glass replenished. And here, again, Mr. Corbet drew his conclusions, from the silent way in which, without a word or a sign from his master, Fletcher gave him more wine continually—wine that was drained off at once.

"Six glasses of sherry before dessert," thought Mr. Corbet to himself. "Bad habit—no wonder Ellinor looks grave." And when the gentlemen were left alone, Mr. Wilkins helped himself even still more freely; yet without the slightest effect on the clearness and brilliancy of his conversation. He had always talked well and racily, that Ralph knew, and in this power he now recognised a temptation to which he feared that his future father-in-law had succumbed. And yet, while he perceived that this gift led into temptation, he coveted it for himself; for he was perfectly aware that this fluency, this happy choice of epithets, was the one thing he should fail in when he began to enter into the more active career of his profession. But after some time spent in listening, and admiring, with this little feeling of envy lurking in the background, Mr. Corbet became aware of Mr. Wilkins's increasing confusion of ideas, and rather unnatural merriment; and, with a sudden revulsion from admiration to disgust, he rose up to go into the library, where Ellinor and Miss Monro were sitting. Mr. Wilkins accompanied him, laughing and talking somewhat loudly. Was Ellinor aware of her father's state? Of that Mr. Corbet could not be sure. She looked up with grave sad eyes as they came into the room, but with no apparent sensation of surprise, annoyance, or shame. When her glance met her father's, Mr. Corbet noticed that it seemed to sober the latter immediately. He sat down near the open window, and did not speak, but sighed heavily from time to time. Miss Monro took up a book, in order to leave the young people to themselves; and after a little low murmured conversation, Ellinor went upstairs to put on her things for a stroll through the meadows by the river-side.

They were sometimes sauntering along in the lovely summer twilight, now resting on some grassy hedge-row bank, or standing still, looking at the great barges, with their crimson sails, lazily floating down the river, making ripples on the glassy opal surface of the water. They did not talk very much; Ellinor seemed disinclined for the exertion; and her lover was thinking over Mr. Wilkins's behaviour, with some surprise and distaste of the habit so evidently growing upon him.

They came home, looking serious and tired: yet they could not account for their fatigue by the length of their walk, and Miss Monro, forgetting Autolycus's song, kept fidgeting about Ellinor, and wondering how it was she looked so pale, if she had only been as far as the Ash Meadow. To escape from this wonder, Ellinor went early to bed. Mr. Wilkins was gone, no one knew where, and Ralph and Miss Monro were left to a half-hour's *tête-à-tête*. He thought he could easily account for Ellinor's languor, if, indeed, she had perceived as much as he had done of her father's state, when they had come into the library after dinner. But there were many details which he was anxious to hear from a comparatively indifferent person, and as soon as he could, he passed on from the conversation about Ellinor's health, to inquiries as to the whole affair of Mr. Dunster's disappearance.

Next to her anxiety about Ellinor, Miss Monro liked to dilate on the mystery connected with Mr. Dunster's flight; for that was the word she employed without hesitation, as she gave him the account of the event universally received and believed in by the people of Hamley. How Mr. Dunster had never been liked by any one; how everybody remembered that he could never look them straight in the face; how he always seemed to be hiding something that he did not want to have known; how he had drawn a large sum (exact quantity unknown) out of the county bank only the day before he left Hamley, doubtless in preparation for his escape; how some one had told Mr. Wilkins he had seen a man just like Dunster lurking about the docks at Liverpool, about two days after he had left his lodgings, but that this some one, being in a hurry, had not cared to stop and speak to the man; how that the affairs in the office were discovered to be in such a sad state that it was no wonder that Mr. Dunster had absconded—he that had been so trusted by poor dear Mr. Wilkins. Money gone no one knew how or where.

"But has he no friends who can explain his proceedings, and account for the missing money, in some way?" asked Mr. Corbet.

"No, none. Mr. Wilkins has written everywhere, right and left, I believe. I know he had a letter from Mr. Dunster's nearest relation—a tradesman in the City—a cousin, I think, and he could give no information in any way. He knew that about ten years ago Mr. Dunster had had a great fancy for going to America, and had read a great many travels—all just what a man would do before going off to a country."

"Ten years is a long time beforehand," said Mr. Corbet, half smiling; "shows malice prepense with a vengeance." But then, turning grave, he said: "Did he leave Hamley in debt?"

"No; I never heard of that," said Miss Monro, rather unwillingly, for she considered it as a piece of loyalty to the Wilkinses, whom Mr. Dunster had injured (as she thought) to blacken his character as much as was consistent with any degree of truth.

"It is a strange story," said Mr. Corbet, musing.

"Not at all," she replied, quickly; "I am sure, if you had seen the man, with one or two side-locks of hair combed over his baldness, as if he were ashamed of it, and his eyes that never looked at you, and his way of eating with his knife when he thought he was not observed—oh, and numbers of things!—you would not think it strange."

Mr. Corbet smiled.

"I only meant that he seems to have had no extravagant or vicious habits which would account for his embezzlement of the money that is missing—but, to be sure, money in itself is a temptation—only he, being a partner, was in a fair way of making it without risk to himself. Has Mr. Wilkins taken any steps to have him arrested in America? He might easily do that."

"Oh, my dear Mr. Ralph, you don't know our good Mr. Wilkins! He would rather bear the loss, I am sure, and all this trouble and care which it has brought upon him, than be revenged upon Mr. Dunster."

"Revenged! What nonsense! It is simple justice—justice to himself and to others—to see that villainy is so sufficiently punished as to deter others from entering upon such courses. But I have little doubt Mr. Wilkins has taken the right steps; he is not the man to sit down quietly under such a loss."

"No, indeed! he had him advertised in the *Times* and in the county papers, and offered a reward of twenty pounds for information concerning him."

"Twenty pounds was too little."

"So I said. I told Ellinor that I would give twenty pounds myself to have him apprehended, and she, poor darling! fell a-trembling, and said, 'I would give all I have—I would give my life.' And then she was in such distress, and sobbed so, I promised her I would never name it to her again."

"Poor child—poor child! she wants change of scene. Her nerves have been sadly shaken by her illness."

The next day was Sunday; Ellinor was to go to church for the first time since her illness. Her father had decided it for her, or else she would fain have stayed away—she would hardly acknowledge why, even to herself, but it seemed to her as if the very words and presence of God must there search her and find her out.

She went early, leaning on the arm of her lover, and trying to forget the past in the present. They walked slowly along between the rows of waving golden corn ripe for the harvest. Mr. Corbet gathered blue and scarlet flowers, and made up a little rustic nosegay for her. She took and stuck it in her girdle, smiling faintly as she did so.

Hamley Church had, in former days, been collegiate, and was, in consequence, much larger and grander than the majority of country-town churches. The Ford Bank pew was a square one, downstairs; the Ford Bank servants sat in a front pew in the gallery, right before their master. Ellinor was "hardening her heart" not to listen, not to hearken to what might disturb the wound which was just being skinned over, when she caught Dixon's face up above. He looked worn, sad, soured, and anxious to a miserable degree; but he was straining eyes and ears, heart and soul, to hear the solemn words read from the pulpit, as if in them alone he could find help in his strait. Ellinor felt rebuked and humbled.

She was in a tumultuous state of mind when they left church; she wished to do her duty, yet could not ascertain what it was. Who was to help her with wisdom and advice? Assuredly he to whom her future life was to be trusted. But the case must be stated in an impersonal form. No one, not even her husband, must ever know anything against her father from her. Ellinor was so artless herself, that she had little idea how quickly and easily some people can penetrate motives, and combine disjointed sentences. She began to speak to Ralph on their slow, sauntering walk homewards through the quiet meadows:

"Suppose, Ralph, that a girl was engaged to be married—"

"I can very easily suppose that, with you by me," said he, filling up her pause.

"Oh! but I don't mean myself at all," replied she, reddening. "I am only thinking of what might happen; and suppose that this girl knew of some one belonging to her—we will call it a brother—who had done something wrong, that would bring disgrace upon the whole family if it was known—though, indeed, it might not have been so very wrong as it seemed, and as it would look to the world—ought she to break off her engagement for fear of involving her lover in the disgrace?"

"Certainly not, without telling him her reason for doing so."

"Ah! but suppose she could not. She might not be at liberty to do so."

"I can't answer supposititious cases. I must have the facts—if facts there are—more plainly before me before I can give an opinion. Who are you thinking of, Ellinor?" asked he, rather abruptly.

"Oh, of no one," she answered in affright. "Why should I be thinking of any one? I often try to plan out what I should do, or what I ought to do, if such and such a thing happened, just as you recollect I used to wonder if I should have presence of mind in case of fire."

"Then, after all, you yourself are the girl who is engaged, and who has the imaginary brother who gets into disgrace?"

"Yes, I suppose so," said she, a little annoyed at having betrayed any personal interest in the affair.

He was silent, meditating.

"There is nothing wrong in it," said she, timidly, "is there?"

"I think you had better tell me fully out what is in your mind," he replied, kindly. "Something has happened which has suggested these questions. Are you putting yourself in the place of any one about whom you have been hearing lately? I know you used to do so formerly, when you were a little girl."

"No; it was a very foolish question of mine, and I ought not to have said anything about it. See! here is Mr. Ness overtaking us."

The clergyman joined them on the broad walk that ran by the river-side, and the talk became general. It was a relief to Ellinor, who had not attained her end, but who had gone far towards betraying something of her own individual interest in the question she had asked. Ralph had been more struck even by her manner than her words. He was sure that something lurked behind, and had an idea of his own that it was connected with Dunster's disappearance. But he was glad that Mr. Ness's joining them gave him leisure to consider a little.

The end of his reflections was, that the next day, Monday, he went into the town, and artfully learnt all he could hear about Mr Dunster's character and mode of going on; and with still more skill he extracted the popular opinion as to the embarrassed nature of Mr. Wilkins's affairs—embarrassment which was generally attributed to Dunster's disappearance with a good large sum belonging to the firm in his possession. But Mr. Corbet thought otherwise; he had accustomed himself to seek out the baser motives for men's conduct, and to call the result of these researches wisdom. He imagined that Dunster had been well paid by Mr. Wilkins for his disappearance, which was an easy way of accounting for the derangement of accounts and loss of money that arose, in fact, from Mr. Wilkins's extravagance of habits and growing intemperance.

On the Monday afternoon he said to Ellinor, "Mr. Ness interrupted us yesterday in a very interesting conversation.   Do you remember, love?"

Ellinor reddened and kept her head still more intently bent over a sketch she was making.

"Yes; I recollect."

"I have been thinking about it. I still think she ought to tell her lover that such disgrace hung over him—I mean, over the family with whom he was going to connect himself. Of course, the only effect would be to make him stand by her still more for her frankness."

"Oh! but, Ralph, it might perhaps be something she ought not to tell, whatever came of her silence."

"Of course there might be all sorts of cases. Unless I knew more I could not pretend to judge."

This was said rather more coolly. It had the desired effect. Ellinor laid down her brush, and covered her face with her hand. After a pause, she turned towards him and said:

"I will tell you this; and more you must not ask me. I know you are as safe as can be. I am the girl, you are the lover, and possible shame hangs over my father, if something—oh, so dreadful" (here she blanched), "but not so very much his fault, is ever found out."

Though this was nothing more than he expected, though Ralph thought that he was aware what the dreadful something might be, yet, when it was acknowledged in words, his heart contracted, and for a moment he forgot the intent, wistful, beautiful face, creeping close to his to read his expression aright. But after that his presence of mind came in aid. He took her in his arms and kissed her; murmuring fond words of sympathy, and promises of faith, nay, even of greater love than before, since greater need she might have of that love. But somehow he was glad when the dressing-bell rang, and in the solitude of his own room he could reflect on what he had heard; for the intelligence had been a great shock to him, although he had fancied that his morning's inquiries had prepared him for it.

CHAPTER IX.

Ralph Corbet found it a very difficult thing to keep down his curiosity during the next few days. It was a miserable thing to have Ellinor's unspoken secret severing them like a phantom. But he had given her his word that he would make no further inquiries from her. Indeed, he thought he could well enough make out the outline of past events; still, there was too much left to conjecture for his mind not to be always busy on the subject. He felt inclined to probe Mr. Wilkins in their after-dinner conversation, in which his host was frank and lax enough on many subjects. But once touch on the name of Dunster and Mr. Wilkins sank into a kind of suspicious depression of spirits; talking little, and with evident caution; and from time to time shooting furtive glances at his interlocutor's face. Ellinor was resolutely impervious to any attempts of his to bring his conversation with her back to the subject which more and more engrossed Ralph Corbet's mind. She had done her duty, as she understood it; and had received assurances which she was only too glad to believe fondly with all the tender faith of her heart. Whatever came to pass, Ralph's love would still be hers; nor was he unwarned of what might come to pass in some dread future day. So she shut her eyes to what might be in store for her (and, after all, the chances were immeasurably in her favour); and she bent herself with her whole strength into enjoying the present. Day by day Mr. Corbet's spirits flagged. He was, however, so generally uniform in the tenor of his talk—never very merry, and always avoiding any subject that might call out deep feeling either on his own or any one else's part, that few people were aware of his changes of mood. Ellinor felt them, though she would not acknowledge them: it was bringing her too much face to face with the great terror of her life.

One morning he announced the fact of his brother's approaching marriage; the wedding was hastened on account of some impending event in the duke's family; and the home letter he had received that day was to bid his presence at Stokely Castle, and also to desire him to be at home by a certain time not very distant, in order to look over the requisite legal papers, and to give his assent to some of them. He gave many reasons why this unlooked-for departure of his was absolutely necessary; but no one doubted it. He need not have alleged such reiterated excuses. The truth was, he was restrained and uncomfortable at Ford Bank ever since Ellinor's confidence. He could not rightly calculate on the most desirable course for his own interests, while his love for her was constantly being renewed by her sweet presence. Away from her, he could judge more wisely. Nor did he allege any false reasons for his departure; but the sense of relief to himself was so great at his recall home, that he was afraid of having it perceived by others; and so took the very way which, if others had been as penetrating as himself, would have betrayed him.

Mr. Wilkins, too, had begun to feel the restraint of Ralph's grave watchful presence. Ellinor was not strong enough to be married; nor was the promised money forthcoming if she had been. And to have a fellow dawdling about the house all day, sauntering into the flower-garden, peering about everywhere, and having a kind of right to put all manner of unexpected questions, was anything but agreeable. It was only Ellinor that clung to his presence—clung as though some shadow of what might happen before they met again had fallen on her spirit. As soon as he had left the house she flew up to a spare bedroom window, to watch for the last glimpse of the fly which was taking him into the town. And then she kissed the part of the pane on which his figure, waving an arm out of the carriage window, had last appeared; and went down slowly to gather together all the things he had last touched—the pen he had mended, the flower he had played with, and to lock them up in the little quaint cabinet that had held her treasures since she was a tiny child.

Miss Monro was, perhaps, very wise in proposing the translation of a difficult part of Dante for a distraction to Ellinor. The girl went meekly, if reluctantly, to the task set her by her good governess, and by-and-by her mind became braced by the exertion.

Ralph's people were not very slow in discovering that something had not gone on quite smoothly with him at Ford Bank. They knew his ways and looks with family intuition, and could easily be certain thus far. But not even his mother's skilfulest wiles, nor his favourite sister's coaxing, could obtain a word or a hint; and when his father, the squire, who had heard the opinions of the female part of the family on this head, began, in his honest blustering way, in their *tête-à-têtes* after dinner, to hope that Ralph was thinking better than to run his head into that confounded Hamley attorney's noose, Ralph gravely required Mr. Corbet to explain his meaning, which he professed not to understand so worded. And when the squire had, with much perplexity, put it into the plain terms of hoping that his son was thinking of breaking off his engagement to Miss Wilkins, Ralph coolly asked him if he was aware that, in that case, he should lose all title to being a man of honour, and might have an action brought against him for breach of promise?

Yet not the less for all this was the idea in his mind as a future possibility.

Before very long the Corbet family moved *en masse* to Stokely Castle for the wedding. Of course, Ralph associated on equal terms with the magnates of the county, who were the employers of Ellinor's father, and spoke of him always as "Wilkins," just as they spoke of the butler as "Simmons." Here, too, among a class of men high above local gossip, and thus unaware of his engagement, he learnt the popular opinion respecting his future father-in-law; an opinion not entirely respectful, though intermingled with a good deal of personal liking. "Poor Wilkins," as they called him, "was sadly extravagant for a man in his position; had no right to spend money, and act as if he were a man of independent fortune." His habits of life were criticised; and pity, not free from blame, was bestowed upon him for the losses he had sustained from his late clerk's disappearance and defalcation. But what could be expected if a man did not choose to attend to his own business?

The wedding went by, as grand weddings do, without let or hindrance, according to the approved pattern. A Cabinet minister honoured it with his presence, and, being a distant relation of the Brabants, remained for a few days after the grand occasion. During this time he became rather intimate with Ralph Corbet; many of their tastes were in common. Ralph took a great interest in the manner of working out political questions; in the balance and state of parties; and had the right appreciation of the exact qualities on which the minister piqued himself. In return, the latter was always on the look-out for promising young men, who, either by their capability of speech-making or article-writing, might advance the views of his party. Recognising the powers he most valued in Ralph, he spared no pains to attach him to his own political set. When they separated, it was with the full understanding that they were to see a good deal of each other in London.

The holiday Ralph allowed himself was passing rapidly away; but, before he returned to his chambers and his hard work, he had promised to spend a few more days with Ellinor; and it suited him to go straight from the duke's to Ford Bank. He left the castle soon after breakfast—the luxurious, elegant breakfast, served by domestics who performed their work with the accuracy and perfection of machines. He arrived at Ford Bank before the man-servant had quite finished the dirtier part of his morning's work, and he came to the glass-door in his striped cotton jacket, a little soiled, and rolling up his working apron. Ellinor was not yet strong enough to get up and go out and gather flowers for the rooms, so those left from yesterday were rather faded; in short, the contrast from entire completeness and exquisite freshness of arrangement struck forcibly upon Ralph's perceptions, which were critical rather than appreciative; and, as his affections were always subdued to his intellect, Ellinor's lovely face and graceful figure flying to meet him did not gain his full approval, because her hair was dressed in an old-fashioned way, her waist was either too long or too short, her sleeves too full or too tight for the standard of fashion to which his eye had been accustomed while scanning the bridesmaids and various highborn ladies at Stokely Castle.

But, as he had always piqued himself upon being able to put on one side all superficial worldliness in his chase after power, it did not do for him to shrink from seeing and facing the incompleteness of moderate means. Only marriage upon moderate means was gradually becoming more distasteful to him.

Nor did his subsequent intercourse with Lord Bolton, the Cabinet minister before mentioned, tend to reconcile him to early matrimony. At Lord Bolton's house he met polished and intellectual society, and all that smoothness in ministering to the lower wants in eating and drinking which seems to provide that the right thing shall always be at the right place at the right time, so that the want of it shall never impede for an instant the feast of wit or reason; while, if he went to the houses of his friends, men of the same college and standing as himself, who had been seduced into early marriages, he was uncomfortably aware of numerous inconsistencies and hitches in their *ménages*. Besides, the idea of the possible disgrace that might befall the family with which he thought of allying himself haunted him with the tenacity and also with the exaggeration of a nightmare, whenever he had overworked himself in his search after available and profitable knowledge, or had a fit of indigestion after the exquisite dinners he was learning so well to appreciate.

Christmas was, of course, to be devoted to his own family; it was an unavoidable necessity, as he told Ellinor, while, in reality, he was beginning to find absence from his betrothed something of a relief. Yet the wranglings and folly of his home, even blessed by the presence of a Lady Maria, made him look forward to Easter at Ford Bank with something of the old pleasure.

Ellinor, with the fine tact which love gives, had discovered his annoyance at various little incongruities in the household at the time of his second visit in the previous autumn, and had laboured to make all as perfect as she could before his return. But she had much to struggle against. For the first time in her life there was a great want of ready money; she could scarcely obtain the servants' wages; and the bill for the spring seeds was a heavy weight on her conscience. For Miss Monro's methodical habits had taught her pupil great exactitude as to all money matters.

Then her father's temper had become very uncertain. He avoided being alone with her whenever he possibly could; and the consciousness of this, and of the terrible mutual secret which was the cause of this estrangement, were the reasons why Ellinor never recovered her pretty youthful bloom after her illness. Of course it was to this that the outside world attributed her changed appearance. They would shake their heads and say, "Ah, poor Miss Wilkins! What a lovely creature she was before that fever!"

But youth is youth, and will assert itself in a certain elasticity of body and spirits; and at times Ellinor forgot that fearful night for several hours together. Even when her father's averted eye brought it all once more before her, she had learnt to form excuses and palliations, and to regard Mr. Dunster's death as only the consequence of an unfortunate accident. But she tried to put the miserable remembrance entirely out of her mind; to go on from day to day thinking only of the day, and how to arrange it so as to cause the least irritation to her father. She would so gladly have spoken to him on the one subject which overshadowed all their intercourse; she fancied that by speaking she might have been able to banish the phantom, or reduce its terror to what she believed to be the due proportion. But her father was evidently determined to show that he was never more to be spoken to on that subject; and all she could do was to follow his lead on the rare occasions that they fell into something like the old confidential intercourse. As yet, to her, he had never given way to anger; but before her he had often spoken in a manner which both pained and terrified her. Sometimes his eye in the midst of his passion caught on her face of affright and dismay, and then he would stop, and make such an effort to control himself as sometimes ended in tears. Ellinor did not understand that both these phases were owing to his increasing habit of drinking more than he ought to have done. She set them down as the direct effects of a sorely burdened conscience; and strove more and more to plan for his daily life at home, how it should go on with oiled wheels, neither a jerk nor a jar. It was no wonder she looked wistful, and careworn, and old. Miss Monro was her great comfort; the total unconsciousness on that lady's part of anything below the surface, and yet her full and delicate recognition of all the little daily cares and trials, made her sympathy most valuable to Ellinor, while there was no need to fear that it would ever give Miss Monro that power of seeing into the heart of things which it frequently confers upon imaginative people, who are deeply attached to some one in sorrow.

There was a strong bond between Ellinor and Dixon, although they scarcely ever exchanged a word save on the most common-place subjects; but their silence was based on different feelings from that which separated Ellinor from her father. Ellinor and Dixon could not speak freely, because their hearts were full of pity for the faulty man whom they both loved so well, and tried so hard to respect.

This was the state of the household to which Ralph Corbet came down at Easter. He might have been known in London as a brilliant diner-out by this time; but he could not afford to throw his life away in fireworks; he calculated his forces, and condensed their power as much as might be, only visiting where he was likely to meet men who could help in his future career. He had been invited to spend the Easter vacation at a certain country house which would be full of such human stepping-stones; and he declined in order to keep his word to Ellinor, and go to Ford Bank. But he could not help looking upon himself a little in the light of a martyr to duty; and perhaps this view of his own merits made him chafe under his future father-in-law's irritability of manner, which now showed itself even to him. He found himself distinctly regretting that he had suffered himself to be engaged so early in life; and having become conscious of the temptation and not having repelled it at once, of course it returned and returned, and gradually obtained the mastery over him. What was to be gained by keeping to his engagement with Ellinor? He should have a delicate wife to look after, and even more than the common additional expenses of married life. He should have a father-in-law whose character at best had had only a local and provincial respectability, which it was now daily losing by habits which were both sensual and vulgarising; a man, too, who was strangely changing from joyous geniality into moody surliness. Besides, he doubted if, in the evident change in the prosperity of the family, the fortune to be paid down on the occasion of his marriage to Ellinor could be forthcoming. And above all, and around all, there hovered the shadow of some unrevealed disgrace, which might come to light at any time and involve him in it. He thought he had pretty well ascertained the nature of this possible shame, and had little doubt it would turn out to be that Dunster's disappearance, to America or elsewhere, had been an arranged plan with Mr. Wilkins. Although Mr. Ralph Corbet was capable of suspecting him of this mean crime (so far removed from the impulsive commission of the past sin which was dragging him daily lower and lower down), it was of a kind that was peculiarly distasteful to the acute lawyer, who foresaw how such base conduct would taint all whose names were ever mentioned, even by chance, in connection with it. He used to lie miserably tossing on his sleepless bed, turning over these things in the night season. He was tormented by all these thoughts; he would bitterly regret the past events that connected him with Ellinor, from the day when he first came to read with Mr. Ness up to the present time. But when he came down in the morning, and saw the faded Ellinor flash into momentary beauty at his entrance into the dining-room, and when she blushingly drew near with the one single flower freshly gathered, which it had been her custom to place in his button-hole when he came down to breakfast, he felt as if his better self was stronger than temptation, and as if he must be an honest man and honourable lover, even against his wish.

As the day wore on the temptation gathered strength. Mr. Wilkins came down, and while he was on the scene Ellinor seemed always engrossed by her father, who apparently cared little enough for all her attentions. Then there was a complaining of the food, which did not suit the sickly palate of a man who had drunk hard the night before; and possibly these complaints were extended to the servants, and their incompleteness or incapacity was thus brought prominently before the eyes of Ralph, who would have preferred to eat a dry crust in silence, or to have gone without breakfast altogether, if he could have had intellectual conversation of some high order, to having the greatest dainties with the knowledge of the care required in their preparation thus coarsely discussed before him. By the time such breakfasts were finished, Ellinor looked thirty, and her spirits were gone for the day. It had become difficult for Ralph to contract his mind to her small domestic interests, and she had little else to talk to him about, now that he responded but curtly to all her questions about himself, and was weary of professing a love which he was ceasing to feel, in all the passionate nothings which usually make up so much of lovers' talk. The books she had been reading were old classics, whose place in literature no longer admitted of keen discussion; the poor whom she cared for were all very well in their way; and, if they could have been brought in to illustrate a theory, hearing about them might have been of some use; but, as it was, it was simply tiresome to hear day after day of Betty Palmer's rheumatism and Mrs. Kay's baby's fits. There was no talking politics with her, because she was so ignorant that she always agreed with everything he said.

He even grew to find luncheon and Miss Monro not unpleasant varieties to his monotonous *tête-à-têtes*. Then came the walk, generally to the town to fetch Mr. Wilkins from his office; and once or twice it was pretty evident how he had been employing his hours. One day in particular his walk was so unsteady and his speech so thick, that Ralph could only wonder how it was that Ellinor did not perceive the cause; but she was too openly anxious about the headache of which her father complained to have been at all aware of the previous self-indulgence which must have brought it on. This very afternoon, as ill-luck would have it, the Duke of Hinton and a gentleman whom Ralph had met in town at Lord Bolton's rode by, and recognised him; saw Ralph supporting a tipsy man with such quiet friendly interest as must show all passers-by that they were previous friends. Mr. Corbet chafed and fumed inwardly all the way home after this unfortunate occurrence; he was in a thoroughly evil temper before they reached Ford Bank, but he had too much self-command to let this be very apparent. He turned into the shrubbery paths, leaving Ellinor to take her father into the quietness of his own room, there to lie down and shake off his headache.

Ralph walked along, ruminating in gloomy mood as to what was to be done; how he could best extricate himself from the miserable relation in which he had placed himself by giving way to impulse. Almost before he was aware, a little hand stole within his folded arms, and Ellinor's sweet sad eyes looked into his.

"I have put papa down for an hour's rest before dinner," said she. "His head seems to ache terribly."

Ralph was silent and unsympathising, trying to nerve himself up to be disagreeable, but finding it difficult in the face of such sweet trust.

"Do you remember our conversation last autumn, Ellinor?" he began at length.

Her head sunk. They were near a garden-seat, and she quietly sat down, without speaking.

"About some disgrace which you then fancied hung over you?" No answer. "Does it still hang over you?"

"Yes!" she whispered, with a heavy sigh.

"And your father knows this, of course?"

"Yes!" again, in the same tone; and then silence.

"I think it is doing him harm," at length Ralph went on, decidedly.

"I am afraid it is," she said, in a low tone.

"I wish you would tell me what it is," he said, a little impatiently. "I might be able to help you about it."

"No! you could not," replied Ellinor. "I was sorry to my very heart to tell you what I did; I did not want help; all that is past. But I wanted to know if you thought that a person situated as I was, was justified in marrying any one ignorant of what might happen, what I do hope and trust never will."

"But if I don't know what you are alluding to in this mysterious way, you must see—don't you see, love?—I am in the position of the ignorant man whom I think you said you could not feel it right to marry. Why don't you tell me straight out what it is?" He could not help his irritation betraying itself in his tones and manner of speaking. She bent a little forward, and looked full into his face, as though to pierce to the very heart's truth of him. Then she said, as quietly as she had ever spoken in her life,—"You wish to break off our engagement?"

He reddened and grew indignant in a moment. "What nonsense! Just because I ask a question and make a remark! I think your illness must have made you fanciful, Ellinor. Surely nothing I said deserves such an interpretation. On the contrary, have I not shown the sincerity and depth of my affection to you by clinging to you through—through everything?"

He was going to say "through the wearying opposition of my family," but he stopped short, for he knew that the very fact of his mother's opposition had only made him the more determined to have his own way in the first instance; and even now he did not intend to let out, what he had concealed up to this time, that his friends all regretted his imprudent engagement.

Ellinor sat silently gazing out upon the meadows, but seeing nothing. Then she put her hand into his. "I quite trust you, Ralph. I was wrong to doubt. I am afraid I have grown fanciful and silly."

He was rather put to it for the right words, for she had precisely divined the dim thought that had overshadowed his mind when she had looked so intently at him. But he caressed her, and reassured her with fond words, as incoherent as lovers' words generally are.

By-and-by they sauntered homewards. When they reached the house, Ellinor left him, and flew up to see how her father was. When Ralph went into his own room he was vexed with himself, both for what he had said and for what he had not said. His mental look-out was not satisfactory.

Neither he nor Mr. Wilkins was in good humour with the world in general at dinner-time, and it needs little in such cases to condense and turn the lowering tempers into one particular direction. As long as Ellinor and Miss Monro stayed in the dining-room, a sort of moody peace had been kept up, the ladies talking incessantly to each other about the trivial nothings of their daily life, with an instinctive consciousness that if they did not chatter on, something would be said by one of the gentlemen which would be distasteful to the other.

As soon as Ralph had shut the door behind them, Mr. Wilkins went to the sideboard, and took out a bottle which had not previously made its appearance.

"Have a little cognac?" he asked, with an assumption of carelessness, as he poured out a wine-glassful. "It's a capital thing for the headache; and this nasty lowering weather has given me a racking headache all day."

"I am sorry for it," said Ralph, "for I wanted particularly to speak to you about business—about my marriage, in fact."

"Well! speak away, I'm as clear-headed as any man, if that's what you mean."

Ralph bowed, a little contemptuously.

"What I wanted to say was, that I am anxious to have all things arranged for my marriage in August. Ellinor is so much better now; in fact, so strong, that I think we may reckon upon her standing the change to a London life pretty well."

Mr. Wilkins stared at him rather blankly, but did not immediately speak.

"Of course I may have the deeds drawn up in which, as by previous arrangement, you advance a certain portion of Ellinor's fortune for the purposes therein to be assigned; as we settled last year when I hoped to have been married in August?"

A thought flitted through Mr. Wilkins's confused brain that he should find it impossible to produce the thousands required without having recourse to the money lenders, who were already making difficulties, and charging him usurious interest for the advances they had lately made; and he unwisely tried to obtain a diminution in the sum he had originally proposed to give Ellinor. "Unwisely," because he might have read Ralph's character better than to suppose he would easily consent to any diminution without good and sufficient reason being given; or without some promise of compensating advantages in the future for the present sacrifice asked from him. But perhaps Mr. Wilkins, dulled as he was by wine thought he could allege a good and sufficient reason, for he said:

"You must not be hard upon me, Ralph. That promise was made before—before I exactly knew the state of my affairs!"

"Before Dunster's disappearance, in fact," said Mr. Corbet, fixing his steady, penetrating eyes on Mr. Wilkins's countenance.

"Yes—exactly—before Dunster's—" mumbled out Mr. Wilkins, red and confused, and not finishing his sentence.

"By the way," said Ralph (for with careful carelessness of manner he thought he could extract something of the real nature of the impending disgrace from his companion, in the state in which he then was; and if he only knew more about this danger he could guard against it; guard others; perhaps himself)—"By the way, have you ever heard anything of Dunster since he went off to—America, isn't it thought?"

He was startled beyond his power of self-control by the instantaneous change in Mr. Wilkins which his question produced. Both started up; Mr. Wilkins white, shaking, and trying to say something, but unable to form a sensible sentence.

"Good God! sir, what is the matter?" said Ralph, alarmed at these signs of physical suffering.

Mr. Wilkins sat down, and repelled his nearer approach without speaking.

"It is nothing, only this headache which shoots through me at times. Don't look at me, sir, in that way. It is very unpleasant to find another man's eyes perpetually fixed upon you."

"I beg your pardon," said Ralph, coldly; his short-lived sympathy, thus repulsed, giving way to his curiosity. But he waited for a minute or two without daring to renew the conversation at the point where they had stopped: whether interrupted by bodily or mental discomfort on the part of his companion he was not quite sure. While he hesitated how to begin again on the subject, Mr. Wilkins pulled the bottle of brandy to himself and filled his glass again, tossing off the spirit as if it had been water. Then he tried to look Mr. Corbet full in the face, with a stare as pertinacious as he could make it, but very different from the keen observant gaze which was trying to read him through.

"What were we talking about?" said Ralph, at length, with the most natural air in the world, just as if he had really been forgetful of some half-discussed subject of interest.

"Of what you'd a d---d deal better hold your tongue about," growled out Mr. Wilkins, in a surly thick voice.

"Sir!" said Ralph, starting to his feet with real passion at being so addressed by "Wilkins the attorney."

"Yes," continued the latter, "I'll manage my own affairs, and allow of no meddling and no questioning. I said so once before, and I was not minded and bad came of it; and now I say it again. And if you're to come here and put impertinent questions, and stare at me as you've been doing this half-hour past, why, the sooner you leave this house the better!"

Ralph half turned to take him at his word, and go at once; but then he "gave Ellinor another chance," as he worded it in his thoughts; but it was in no spirit of conciliation that he said:

"You've taken too much of that stuff, sir. You don't know what you're saying. If you did, I should leave your house at once, never to return."

"You think so, do you?" said Mr. Wilkins, trying to stand up, and look dignified and sober. "I say, sir, that if you ever venture again to talk and look as you have done to-night, why, sir, I will ring the bell and have you shown the door by my servants. So now you're warned, my fine fellow!" He sat down, laughing a foolish tipsy laugh of triumph. In another minute his arm was held firmly but gently by Ralph.

"Listen, Mr. Wilkins," he said, in a low hoarse voice. "You shall never have to say to me twice what you have said to-night. Henceforward we are as strangers to each other. As to Ellinor"—his tones softened a little, and he sighed in spite of himself—"I do not think we should have been happy. I believe our engagement was formed when we were too young to know our own minds, but I would have done my duty and kept to my word; but you, sir, have yourself severed the connection between us by your insolence to-night. I, to be turned out of your house by your servants!—I, a Corbet of Westley, who would not submit to such threats from a peer of the realm, let him be ever so drunk!" He was out of the room, almost out of the house, before he had spoken the last words.

Mr. Wilkins sat still, first fiercely angry, then astonished, and lastly dismayed into sobriety. "Corbet, Corbet! Ralph!" he called in vain; then he got up and went to the door, opened it, looked into the fully-lighted hall; all was so quiet there that he could hear the quiet voices of the women in the drawing-room talking together. He thought for a moment, went to the hat-stand, and missed Ralph's low-crowned straw hat.

Then he sat down once more in the dining-room, and endeavoured to make out exactly what had passed; but he could not believe that Mr. Corbet had come to any enduring or final resolution to break off his engagement, and he had almost reasoned himself back into his former state of indignation at impertinence and injury, when Ellinor came in, pale, hurried, and anxious.

"Papa! what does this mean?" said she, putting an open note into his hand. He took up his glasses, but his hand shook so that he could hardly read. The note was from the Parsonage, to Ellinor; only three lines sent by Mr. Ness's servant, who had come to fetch Mr. Corbet's things. He had written three lines with some consideration for Ellinor, even when he was in his first flush of anger against her father, and it must be confessed of relief at his own freedom, thus brought about by the act of another, and not of his own working out, which partly saved his conscience. The note ran thus:

"DEAR ELLINOR,—Words have passed between your father and me which have obliged me to leave his house, I fear, never to return to it. I will write more fully to-morrow. But do not grieve too much, for I am not, and never have been, good enough for you. God bless you, my dearest Nelly, though I call you so for the last time.—R. C."

"Papa, what is it?" Ellinor cried, clasping her hands together, as her father sat silent, vacantly gazing into the fire, after finishing the note.

"I don't know!" said he, looking up at her piteously; "it's the world, I think. Everything goes wrong with me and mine: it went wrong before THAT night—so it can't be that, can it, Ellinor?"

"Oh, papa!" said she, kneeling down by him, her face hidden on his breast.

He put one arm languidly round her. "I used to read of Orestes and the Furies at Eton when I was a boy, and I thought it was all a heathen fiction. Poor little motherless girl!" said he, laying his other hand on her head, with the caressing gesture he had been accustomed to use when she had been a little child. "Did you love him so very dearly, Nelly?" he whispered, his cheek against her: "for somehow of late he has not seemed to me good enough for thee. He has got an inkling that something has gone wrong, and he was very inquisitive—I may say he questioned me in a relentless kind of way."

"Oh, papa, it was my doing, I'm afraid. I said something long ago about possible disgrace."

He pushed her away; he stood up, and looked at her with the eyes dilated, half in fear, half in fierceness, of an animal at bay; he did not heed that his abrupt movement had almost thrown her prostrate on the ground.

"You, Ellinor! You—you—"

"Oh, darling father, listen!" said she, creeping to his knees, and clasping them with her hands. "I said it, as if it were a possible case, of some one else—last August—but he immediately applied it, and asked me if it was over me the disgrace, or shame—I forget the words we used—hung; and what could I say?"

"Anything—anything to put him off the scent. God help me, I am a lost man, betrayed by my child!"

Ellinor let go his knees, and covered her face. Every one stabbed at that poor heart. In a minute or so her father spoke again.

"I don't mean what I say. I often don't mean it now. Ellinor, you must forgive me, my child!" He stooped, and lifted her up, and sat down, taking her on his knee, and smoothing her hair off her hot forehead. "Remember, child, how very miserable I am, and have forgiveness for me. He had none, and yet he must have seen I had been drinking."

"Drinking, papa!" said Ellinor, raising her head, and looking at him with sorrowful surprise.

"Yes. I drink now to try and forget," said he, blushing and confused.

"Oh, how miserable we are!" cried Ellinor, bursting into tears—"how very miserable! It seems almost as if God had forgotten to comfort us!"

"Hush! hush!" said he. "Your mother said once she did so pray that you might grow up religious; you must be religious, child, because she prayed for it so often. Poor Lettice, how glad I am that you are dead!" Here he began to cry like a child. Ellinor comforted him with kisses rather than words. He pushed her away, after a while, and said, sharply: "How much does he know? I must make sure of that. How much did you tell him, Ellinor?"

"Nothing—nothing, indeed, papa, but what I told you just now!"

"Tell it me again—the exact words!"

"I will, as well as I can; but it was last August. I only said, 'Was it right for a woman to marry, knowing that disgrace hung over her, and keeping her lover in ignorance of it?'"

"That was all, you are sure?"

"Yes. He immediately applied the case to me—to ourselves."

"And he never wanted to know what was the nature of the threatened disgrace?"

"Yes, he did."

"And you told him?"

"No, not a word more. He referred to the subject again to-day, in the shrubbery; but I told him nothing more. You quite believe me, don't you, papa?"

He pressed her to him, but did not speak. Then he took the note up again, and read it with as much care and attention as he could collect in his agitated state of mind.

"Nelly," said he, at length, "he says true; he is not good enough for thee. He shrinks from the thought of the disgrace. Thou must stand alone, and bear the sins of thy father."

He shook so much as he said this, that Ellinor had to put any suffering of her own on one side, and try to confine her thoughts to the necessity of getting her father immediately up to bed. She sat by him till he went to sleep, and she could leave him, and go to her own room, to forgetfulness and rest, if she could find those priceless blessings.

CHAPTER X.

Mr. Corbet was so well known at the Parsonage by the two old servants, that he had no difficulty, on reaching it, after his departure from Ford Bank, in having the spare bed-chamber made ready for him, late as it was, and in the absence of the master, who had taken a little holiday, now that Lent and Easter were over, for the purpose of fishing. While his room was getting ready, Ralph sent for his clothes, and by the same messenger he despatched the little note to Ellinor. But there was the letter he had promised her in it still to be written; and it was almost his night's employment to say enough, yet not too much; for, as he expressed it to himself, he was half way over the stream, and it would be folly to turn back, for he had given nearly as much pain both to himself and Ellinor by this time as he should do by making the separation final. Besides, after Mr. Wilkins's speeches that evening—but he was candid enough to acknowledge that, bad and offensive as they had been, if they had stood alone they might have been condoned.

His letter ran as follows:

"DEAREST ELLINOR, for dearest you are, and I think will ever be, my judgment has consented to a step which is giving me great pain, greater than you will readily believe. I am convinced that it is better that we should part; for circumstances have occurred since we formed our engagement which, although I am unaware of their exact nature, I can see weigh heavily upon you, and have materially affected your father's behaviour. Nay, I think, after to-night, I may almost say have entirely altered his feelings towards me. What these circumstances are I am ignorant, any further than that I know from your own admission, that they may lead to some future disgrace. Now, it may be my fault, it may be in my temperament, to be anxious, above all things earthly, to obtain and possess a high reputation. I can only say that it is so, and leave you to blame me for my weakness as much as you like. But anything that might come in between me and this object would, I own, be ill tolerated by me; the very dread of such an obstacle intervening would paralyse me. I should become irritable, and, deep as my affection is, and always must be, towards you, I could not promise you a happy, peaceful life. I should be perpetually haunted by the idea of what might happen in the way of discovery and shame. I am the more convinced of this from my observation of your father's altered character—an alteration which I trace back to the time when I conjecture that the secret affairs took place to which you have alluded. In short, it is for your sake, my dear Ellinor, even more than for my own, that I feel compelled to affix a final meaning to the words which your father addressed to me last night, when he desired me to leave his house for ever. God bless you, my Ellinor, for the last time my Ellinor. Try to forget as soon as you can the unfortunate tie which has bound you for a time to one so unsuitable—I believe I ought to say so unworthy of you—as—RALPH CORBET."

Ellinor was making breakfast when this letter was given her. According to the wont of the servants of the respective households of the Parsonage and Ford Bank, the man asked if there was any answer. It was only custom; for he had not been desired to do so. Ellinor went to the window to read her letter; the man waiting all the time respectfully for her reply. She went to the writing-table, and wrote:

"It is all right—quite right. I ought to have thought of it all last August. I do not think you will forget me easily, but I entreat you never at any future time to blame yourself. I hope you will be happy and successful. I suppose I must never write to you again: but I shall always pray for you. Papa was very sorry last night for having spoken angrily to you. You must forgive him—there is great need for forgiveness in this world.—ELLINOR."

She kept putting down thought after thought, just to prolong the last pleasure of writing to him. She sealed the note, and gave it to the man. Then she sat down and waited for Miss Monro, who had gone to bed on the previous night without awaiting Ellinor's return from the dining-room.

"I am late, my dear," said Miss Monro, on coming down, "but I have a bad headache, and I knew you had a pleasant companion." Then, looking round, she perceived Ralph's absence.

"Mr. Corbet not down yet!" she exclaimed. And then Ellinor had to tell her the outline of the facts so soon likely to be made public; that Mr. Corbet and she had determined to break off their engagement; and that Mr. Corbet had accordingly betaken himself to the Parsonage; and that she did not expect him to return to Ford Bank. Miss Monro's astonishment was unbounded. She kept going over and over all the little circumstances she had noticed during the last visit, only on yesterday, in fact, which she could not reconcile with the notion that the two, apparently so much attached to each other but a few hours before, were now to be for ever separated and estranged. Ellinor sickened under the torture; which yet seemed like torture in a dream, from which there must come an awakening and a relief. She felt as if she could not hear any more; yet there was more to hear. Her father, as it turned out, was very ill, and had been so all night long; he had evidently had some kind of attack on the brain, whether apoplectic or paralytic it was for the doctors to decide. In the hurry and anxiety of this day of misery succeeding to misery, she almost forgot to wonder whether Ralph were still at the Parsonage—still in Hamley; it was not till the evening visit of the physician that she learnt that he had been seen by Dr. Moore as he was taking his place in the morning mail to London. Dr. Moore alluded to his name as to a thought that would cheer and comfort the fragile girl during her night-watch by her father's bedside. But Miss Monro stole out after the doctor to warn him off the subject for the future, crying bitterly over the forlorn position of her darling as she spoke—crying as Ellinor had never yet been able to cry: though all the time, in the pride of her sex, she was as endeavouring to persuade the doctor it was entirely Ellinor's doing, and the wisest and best thing she could have done, as he was not good enough for her, only a poor barrister struggling for a livelihood. Like many other kind-hearted people, she fell into the blunder of lowering the moral character of those whom it is their greatest wish to exalt. But Dr. Moore knew Ellinor too well to believe the whole of what Miss Monro said; she would never act from interested motives, and was all the more likely to cling to a man because he was down and unsuccessful. No! there had been a lovers' quarrel; and it could not have happened at a sadder time.

Before the June roses were in full bloom, Mr. Wilkins was dead. He had left his daughter to the guardianship of Mr. Ness by some will made years ago; but Mr. Ness had caught a rheumatic fever with his Easter fishings, and been unable to be moved home from the little Welsh inn where he had been staying when he was taken ill. Since his last attack, Mr. Wilkins's mind had been much affected; he often talked strangely and wildly; but he had rare intervals of quietness and full possession of his senses. At one of these times he must have written a half-finished pencil note, which his nurse found under his pillow after his death, and brought to Ellinor. Through her tear-blinded eyes she read the weak, faltering words:

"I am very ill. I sometimes think I shall never get better, so I wish to ask your pardon for what I said the night before I was taken ill. I am afraid my anger made mischief between you and Ellinor, but I think you will forgive a dying man. If you will come back and let all be as it used to be, I will make any apology you may require. If I go, she will be so very friendless; and I have looked to you to care for her ever since you first—" Then came some illegible and incoherent writing, ending with, "From my deathbed I adjure you to stand her friend; I will beg pardon on my knees for anything—"

And there strength had failed; the paper and pencil had been laid aside to be resumed at some time when the brain was clearer, the hand stronger. Ellinor kissed the letter, reverently folded it up, and laid it among her sacred treasures, by her mother's half-finished sewing, and a little curl of her baby sister's golden hair.

Mr. Johnson, who had been one of the trustees for Mrs. Wilkins's marriage settlement, a respectable solicitor in the county town, and Mr. Ness, had been appointed executors of his will, and guardians to Ellinor. The will itself had been made several years before, when he imagined himself the possessor of a handsome fortune, the bulk of which he bequeathed to his only child. By her mother's marriage-settlement, Ford Bank was held in trust for the children of the marriage; the trustees being Sir Frank Holster and Mr. Johnson. There were legacies to his executors; a small annuity to Miss Monro, with the expression of a hope that it might be arranged for her to continue living with Ellinor as long as the latter remained unmarried; all his servants were remembered, Dixon especially, and most liberally.

What remained of the handsome fortune once possessed by the testator? The executors asked in vain; there was nothing. They could hardly make out what had become of it, in such utter confusion were all the accounts, both personal and official. Mr. Johnson was hardly restrained by his compassion for the orphan from throwing up the executorship in disgust. Mr. Ness roused himself from his scholarlike abstraction to labour at the examination of books, parchments, and papers, for Ellinor's sake. Sir Frank Holster professed himself only a trustee for Ford Bank.

Meanwhile she went on living at Ford Bank, quite unconscious of the state of her father's affairs, but sunk into a deep, plaintive melancholy, which affected her looks and the tones of her voice in such a manner as to distress Miss Monro exceedingly. It was not that the good lady did not quite acknowledge the great cause her pupil had for grieving—deserted by her lover, her father dead—but that she could not bear the outward signs of how much these sorrows had told on Ellinor. Her love for the poor girl was infinitely distressed by seeing the daily wasting away, the constant heavy depression of spirits, and she grew impatient of the continual pain of sympathy. If Miss Monro could have done something to relieve Ellinor of her woe, she would have been less inclined to scold her for giving way to it.

The time came when Miss Monro could act; and after that, there was no more irritation on her part. When all hope of Ellinor's having anything beyond the house and grounds of Ford Bank was gone; when it was proved that all the legacies bequeathed by Mr. Wilkins not one farthing could ever be paid; when it came to be a question how far the beautiful pictures and other objects of art in the house were not legally the property of unsatisfied creditors, the state of her father's affairs was communicated to Ellinor as delicately as Mr. Ness knew how.

She was drooping over her work—she always drooped now—and she left off sewing to listen to him, leaning her head on the arm which rested on the table. She did not speak when he had ended his statement. She was silent for whole minutes afterwards; he went on speaking out of very agitation and awkwardness.

"It was all the rascal Dunster's doing, I've no doubt," said he, trying to account for the entire loss of Mr. Wilkins's fortune.

To his surprise she lifted up her white stony face, and said slowly and faintly, but with almost solemn calmness:

"Mr. Ness, you must never allow Mr. Dunster to be blamed for this!"

"My dear Ellinor, there can be no doubt about it. Your father himself always referred to the losses he had sustained by Dunster's disappearance."

Ellinor covered her face with her hands. "God forgive us all," she said, and relapsed into the old unbearable silence. Mr. Ness had undertaken to discuss her future plans with her, and he was obliged to go on.

"Now, my dear child—I have known you since you were quite a little girl, you know—we must try not to give way to feeling"—he himself was choking; she was quite quiet—"but think what is to be done. You will have the rent of this house, and we have a very good offer for it—a tenant on lease of seven years at a hundred and twenty pounds a year—"

"I will never let this house," said she, standing up suddenly, and as if defying him.

"Not let Ford Bank! Why? I don't understand it—I can't have been clear—Ellinor, the rent of this house is all you will have to live on!"

"I can't help it, I can't leave this house. Oh, Mr. Ness, I can't leave this house."

"My dear child, you shall not be hurried—I know how hardly all these things are coming upon you (and I wish I had never seen Corbet, with all my heart I do!)"—this was almost to himself, but she must have heard it, for she quivered all over—"but leave this house you must. You must eat, and the rent of this house must pay for your food; you must dress, and there is nothing but the rent to clothe you. I will gladly have you to stay at the Parsonage as long as ever you like; but, in fact, the negotiations with Mr. Osbaldistone, the gentleman who offers to take the house, are nearly completed—"

"It is my house!" said Ellinor, fiercely. "I know it is settled on me."

"No, my dear. It is held in trust for you by Sir Frank Holster and Mr. Johnson; you to receive all moneys and benefits accruing from it"—he spoke gently, for he almost thought her head was turned—"but you remember you are not of age, and Mr. Johnson and I have full power."

Ellinor sat down, helpless.

"Leave me," she said, at length. "You are very kind, but you don't know all. I cannot stand any more talking now," she added, faintly.

Mr. Ness bent over her and kissed her forehead, and withdrew without another word. He went to Miss Monro.

"Well! and how did you find her?" was her first inquiry, after the usual greetings had passed between them. "It is really quite sad to see how she gives way; I speak to her, and speak to her, and tell her how she is neglecting all her duties, and it does no good."

"She has had to bear a still further sorrow to-day," said Mr. Ness. "On the part of Mr. Johnson and myself I have a very painful duty to perform to you as well as to her. Mr. Wilkins has died insolvent. I grieve to say there is no hope of your ever receiving any of your annuity!"

Miss Monro looked very blank. Many happy little visions faded away in those few moments; then she roused up and said, "I am but forty; I have a good fifteen years of work in me left yet, thank God. Insolvent! Do you mean he has left no money?"

"Not a farthing. The creditors may be thankful if they are fully paid."

"And Ellinor?"

"Ellinor will have the rent of this house, which is hers by right of her mother's settlement, to live on."

"How much will that be?"

"One hundred and twenty pounds."

Miss Monro's lips went into a form prepared for whistling. Mr. Ness continued:

"She is at present unwilling enough to leave this house, poor girl. It is but natural; but she has no power in the matter, even were there any other course open to her. I can only say how glad, how honoured, I shall feel by as long a visit as you and she can be prevailed upon to pay me at the Parsonage."

"Where is Mr. Corbet?" said Miss Monro.

"I do not know. After breaking off his engagement he wrote me a long letter, explanatory, as he called it; exculpatory, as I termed it. I wrote back, curtly enough, saying that I regretted the breaking-off of an intercourse which had always been very pleasant to me, but that he must be aware that, with my intimacy with the family at Ford Bank, it would be both awkward and unpleasant to all parties if he and I remained on our previous footing. Who is that going past the window? Ellinor riding?"

Miss Monro went to the window. "Yes! I am thankful to see her on horseback again. It was only this morning I advised her to have a ride!"

"Poor Dixon! he will suffer too; his legacy can no more be paid than the others; and it is not many young ladies who will be as content to have so old-fashioned a groom riding after them as Ellinor seems to be."

As soon as Mr. Ness had left, Miss Monro went to her desk and wrote a long letter to some friends she had at the cathedral town of East Chester, where she had spent some happy years of her former life. Her thoughts had gone back to this time even while Mr. Ness had been speaking; for it was there her father had lived, and it was after his death that her cares in search of a subsistence had begun. But the recollections of the peaceful years spent there were stronger than the remembrance of the weeks of sorrow and care; and, while Ellinor's marriage had seemed a probable event, she had made many a little plan of returning to her native place, and obtaining what daily teaching she could there meet with, and the friends to whom she was now writing had promised her their aid. She thought that as Ellinor had to leave Ford Bank, a home at a distance might be more agreeable to her, and she went on to plan that they should live together, if possible, on her earnings, and the small income that would be Ellinor's. Miss Monro loved her pupil so dearly, that, if her own pleasure only were to be consulted, this projected life would be more agreeable to her than if Mr. Wilkins's legacy had set her in independence, with Ellinor away from her, married, and with interests in which her former governess had but little part.

As soon as Mr. Ness had left her, Ellinor rang the bell, and startled the servant who answered it by her sudden sharp desire to have the horses at the door as soon as possible, and to tell Dixon to be ready to go out with her.

She felt that she must speak to him, and in her nervous state she wanted to be out on the free broad common, where no one could notice or remark their talk. It was long since she had ridden, and much wonder was excited by the sudden movement in kitchen and stable-yard. But Dixon went gravely about his work of preparation, saying nothing.

They rode pretty hard till they reached Monk's Heath, six or seven miles away from Hamley. Ellinor had previously determined that here she would talk over the plan Mr. Ness had proposed to her with Dixon, and he seemed to understand her without any words passing between them. When she reined in he rode up to her, and met the gaze of her sad eyes with sympathetic, wistful silence.

"Dixon," said she, "they say I must leave Ford Bank."

"I was afeared on it, from all I've heerd say i' the town since the master's death."

"Then you've heard—then you know—that papa has left hardly any money—my poor dear Dixon, you won't have your legacy, and I never thought of that before!"

"Never heed, never heed," said he, eagerly; "I couldn't have touched it if it had been there, for the taking it would ha' seemed too like—" Blood-money, he was going to say, but he stopped in time. She guessed the meaning, though not the word he would have used.

"No, not that," said she; "his will was dated years before. But oh, Dixon, what must I do? They will make me leave Ford Bank, I see. I think the trustees have half let it already."

"But you'll have the rent on't, I reckon?" asked he, anxiously. "I've many a time heerd 'em say as it was settled on the missus first, and then on you."

"Oh, yes, it is not that; but you know, under the beech-tree—"

"Ay!" said he, heavily. "It's been oftentimes on my mind, waking, and I think there's ne'er a night as I don't dream of it."

"But how can I leave it!" Ellinor cried. "They may do a hundred things—may dig up the shrubbery. Oh! Dixon, I feel as if it was sure to be found out! Oh! Dixon, I cannot bear any more blame on papa—it will kill me—and such a dreadful thing, too!"

Dixon's face fell into the lines of habitual pain that it had always assumed of late years whenever he was thinking or remembering anything.

"They must ne'er ha' reason to speak ill of the dead, that's for certain," said he. "The Wilkinses have been respected in Hamley all my lifetime, and all my father's before me, and—surely, missy, there's ways and means of tying tenants up from alterations both in the house and out of it, and I'd beg the trustees, or whatever they's called, to be very particular, if I was you, and not have a thing touched either in the house, or the gardens, or the meadows, or the stables. I think, wi' a word from you, they'd maybe keep me on i' the stables, and I could look after things a bit; and the Day o' Judgment will come at last, when all our secrets will be made known wi'out our having the trouble and the shame o' telling 'em. I'm getting rayther tired o' this world, Miss Ellinor."

"Don't talk so," said Ellinor, tenderly. "I know how sad it is, but, oh! remember how I shall want a friend when you're gone, to advise me as you have done to-day. You're not feeling ill, Dixon, are you?" she continued, anxiously.

"No! I'm hearty enough, and likely for t' live. Father was eighty-one, and mother above the seventies, when they died. It's only my heart as is got to feel so heavy; and as for that matter, so is yours, I'll be bound. And it's a comfort to us both if we can serve him as is dead by any care of ours, for he were such a bright handsome lad, with such a cheery face, as never should ha' known shame."

They rode on without much more speaking. Ellinor was silently planning for Dixon, and he, not caring to look forward to the future, was bringing up before his fancy the time, thirty years ago, when he had first entered the elder Mr. Wilkins's service as stable-lad, and pretty Molly, the scullery-maid, was his daily delight. Pretty Molly lay buried in Hamley churchyard, and few living, except Dixon, could have gone straight to her grave.

CHAPTER XI.

In a few days Miss Monro obtained a most satisfactory reply to her letter of inquiries as to whether a daily governess could find employment in East Chester. For once the application seemed to have come just at the right time. The canons were most of them married men, with young families; those at present in residence welcomed the idea of such instruction as Miss Monro could offer for their children, and could almost answer for their successors in office. This was a great step gained. Miss Monro, the daughter of a precentor to this very cathedral, had a secret unwillingness to being engaged as a teacher by any wealthy tradesman there; but to be received into the canons' families, in almost any capacity, was like going home. Moreover, besides the empty honour of the thing, there were many small pieces of patronage in the gift of the Chapter—such as a small house opening on to the Close, which had formerly belonged to the verger, but which was now vacant, and was offered to Miss Monro at a nominal rent.

Ellinor had once more sunk into her old depressed passive state; Mr. Ness and Miss Monro, modest and undecided as they both were in general, had to fix and arrange everything for her. Her great interest seemed to be in the old servant Dixon, and her great pleasure to lie in seeing him, and talking over old times; so her two friends talked about her, little knowing what a bitter, stinging pain her "pleasure" was. In vain Ellinor tried to plan how they could take Dixon with them to East Chester. If he had been a woman it would have been a feasible step; but they were only to keep one servant, and Dixon, capable and versatile as he was, would not do for that servant. All this was what passed through Ellinor's mind: it is still a question whether Dixon would have felt his love of his native place, with all its associations and remembrances, or his love for Ellinor, the stronger. But he was not put to the proof; he was only told that he must leave, and seeing Ellinor's extreme grief at the idea of their separation, he set himself to comfort her by every means in his power, reminding her, with tender choice of words, how necessary it was that he should remain on the spot, in Mr. Osbaldistone's service, in order to frustrate, by any small influence he might have, every project of alteration in the garden that contained the dreadful secret. He persisted in this view, though Ellinor repeated, with pertinacious anxiety, the care which Mr. Johnson had taken, in drawing up the lease, to provide against any change or alteration being made in the present disposition of the house or grounds.

People in general were rather astonished at the eagerness Miss Wilkins showed to sell all the Ford Bank furniture. Even Miss Monro was a little scandalized at this want of sentiment, although she said nothing about it; indeed justified the step, by telling every one how wisely Ellinor was acting, as the large, handsome, tables and chairs would be very much out of place and keeping with the small, oddly-shaped rooms of their future home in East Chester Close. None knew how strong was the instinct of self-preservation, it may almost be called, which impelled Ellinor to shake off, at any cost of present pain, the incubus of a terrible remembrance. She wanted to go into an unhaunted dwelling in a free, unknown country—she felt as if it was her only chance of sanity. Sometimes she thought her senses would not hold together till the time when all these arrangements were ended. But she did not speak to any one about her feelings, poor child; to whom could she speak on the subject but to Dixon? Nor did she define them to herself. All she knew was, that she was as nearly going mad as possible; and if she did, she feared that she might betray her father's guilt. All this time she never cried, or varied from her dull, passive demeanour. And they were blessed tears of relief that she shed when Miss Monro, herself weeping bitterly, told her to put her head out of the post-chaise window, for at the next turning of the road they would catch the last glimpse of Hamley church spire.

Late one October evening, Ellinor had her first sight of East Chester Close, where she was to pass the remainder of her life. Miss Monro had been backwards and forwards between Hamley and East Chester more than once, while Ellinor remained at the parsonage; so she had not only the pride of proprietorship in the whole of the beautiful city, but something of the desire of hospitably welcoming Ellinor to their joint future home.

"Look! the fly must take us a long round, because of our luggage; but behind these high old walls are the canons' gardens. That high-pitched roof, with the clumps of stonecrop on the walls near it, is Canon Wilson's, whose four little girls I am to teach. Hark! the great cathedral clock. How proud I used to be of its great boom when I was a child! I thought all the other church clocks in the town sounded so shrill and poor after that, which I considered mine especially. There are rooks flying home to the elms in the Close. I wonder if they are the same that used to be there when I was a girl. They say the rook is a very long-lived bird, and I feel as if I could swear to the way they are cawing. Ay, you may smile, Ellinor, but I understand now those lines of Gray's you used to say so prettily—

"I feel the gales that from ye blow.
A momentary bliss bestow,

And breathe a second spring."

Now, dear, you must get out. This flagged walk leads to our front-door; but our back rooms, which are the pleasantest, look on to the Close, and the cathedral, and the lime-tree walk, and the deanery, and the rookery."

It was a mere slip of a house; the kitchen being wisely placed close to the front-door, and so reserving the pretty view for the little dining-room, out of which a glass-door opened into a small walled-in garden, which had again an entrance into the Close. Upstairs was a bedroom to the front, which Miss Monro had taken for herself, because as she said, she had old associations with the back of every house in the High-street, while Ellinor mounted to the pleasant chamber above the tiny drawing-room both of which looked on to the vast and solemn cathedral, and the peaceful dignified Close. East Chester Cathedral is Norman, with a low, massive tower, a grand, majestic nave, and a choir full of stately historic tombs. The whole city is so quiet and decorous a place, that the perpetual daily chants and hymns of praise seemed to sound far and wide over the roofs of the houses. Ellinor soon became a regular attendant at all the morning and evening services. The sense of worship calmed and soothed her aching weary heart, and to be punctual to the cathedral hours she roused and exerted herself, when probably nothing else would have been sufficient to this end.

By-and-by Miss Monro formed many acquaintances; she picked up, or was picked up by, old friends, and the descendants of old friends. The grave and kindly canons, whose children she taught, called upon her with their wives, and talked over the former deans and chapters, of whom she had both a personal and traditional knowledge, and as they walked away and talked about her silent delicate-looking friend Miss Wilkins, and perhaps planned some little present out of their fruitful garden or bounteous stores, which should make Miss Monro's table a little more tempting to one apparently so frail as Ellinor, for the household was always spoken of as belonging to Miss Monro, the active and prominent person. By-and-by, Ellinor herself won her way to their hearts, not by words or deeds, but by her sweet looks and meek demeanour, as they marked her regular attendance at cathedral service: and when they heard of her constant visits to a certain parochial school, and of her being sometimes seen carrying a little covered basin to the cottages of the poor, they began to try and tempt her, with more urgent words, to accompany Miss Monro in her frequent tea-drinkings at their houses. The old dean, that courteous gentleman and good Christian, had early become great friends with Ellinor. He would watch at the windows of his great vaulted library till he saw her emerge from the garden into the Close, and then open the deanery door, and join her, she softly adjusting the measure of her pace to his. The time of his departure from East Chester became a great blank in her life, although she would never accept, or allow Miss Monro to accept, his repeated invitations to go and pay him a visit at his country-place. Indeed, having once tasted comparative peace again in East Chester Cathedral Close, it seemed as though she was afraid of ever venturing out of those calm precincts. All Mr. Ness's invitations to visit him at his parsonage at Hamley were declined, although he was welcomed at Miss Monro's, on the occasion of his annual visit, by every means in their power. He slept at one of the canon's vacant houses, and lived with his two friends, who made a yearly festivity, to the best of their means, in his honour, inviting such of the cathedral clergy as were in residence: or, if they failed, condescending to the town clergy. Their friends knew well that no presents were so acceptable as those sent while Mr. Ness was with them; and from the dean, who would send them a hamper of choice fruit and flowers from Oxton Park, down to the curate, who worked in the same schools as Ellinor, and who was a great fisher, and caught splendid trout—all did their best to help them to give a welcome to the only visitor they ever had. The only visitor they ever had, as far as the stately gentry knew. There was one, however, who came as often as his master could give him a holiday long enough to undertake a journey to so distant a place; but few knew of his being a guest at Miss Monro's, though his welcome there was not less hearty than Mr. Ness's—this was Dixon. Ellinor had convinced him that he could give her no greater pleasure at any time than by allowing her to frank him to and from East Chester. Whenever he came they were together the greater part of the day; she taking him hither and thither to see all the sights that she thought would interest or please him; but they spoke very little to each other during all this companionship. Miss Monro had much more to say to him. She questioned him right and left whenever Ellinor was out of the room. She learnt that the house at Ford Bank was splendidly furnished, and no money spared on the garden; that the eldest Miss Hanbury was very well married; that Brown had succeeded to Jones in the haberdasher's shop. Then she hesitated a little before making her next inquiry:

"I suppose Mr. Corbet never comes to the Parsonage now?"

"No, not he. I don't think as how Mr. Ness would have him; but they write letters to each other by times. Old Job—you'll recollect old Job, ma'am, he that gardened for Mr Ness, and waited in the parlour when there was company—did say as one day he heerd them speaking about Mr. Corbet; and he's a grand counsellor now—one of them as goes about at assize-time, and speaks in a wig."

"A barrister, you mean," said Miss Monro.

"Ay; and he's something more than that, though I can't rightly remember what,"

Ellinor could have told them both. They had *The Times* lent to them on the second day after publication by one of their friends in the Close, and Ellinor, watching till Miss Monro's eyes were otherwise engaged, always turned with trembling hands and a beating heart to the reports of the various courts of law. In them she found—at first rarely—the name she sought for, the name she dwelt upon, as if every letter were a study. Mr. Losh and Mr. Duncombe appeared for the plaintiff, Mr. Smythe and Mr. Corbet for the defendant. In a year or two that name appeared more frequently, and generally took the precedence of the other, whatever it might be; then on special occasions his speeches were reported at full length, as if his words were accounted weighty; and by-and-by she saw that he had been appointed a Queen's counsel. And this was all she ever heard or saw about him; his once familiar name never passed her lips except in hurried whispers to Dixon, when he came to stay with them. Ellinor had had no idea when she parted from Mr. Corbet how total the separation between them was henceforward to be, so much seemed left unfinished, unexplained. It was so difficult, at first, to break herself of the habit of constant mental reference to him; and for many a long year she kept thinking that surely some kind fortune would bring them together again, and all this heart-sickness and melancholy estrangement from each other would then seem to both only as an ugly dream that had passed away in the morning light.

The dean was an old man, but there was a canon who was older still, and whose death had been expected by many, and speculated upon by some, any time for ten years at least. Canon Holdsworth was too old to show active kindness to any one; the good dean's life was full of thoughtful and benevolent deeds. But he was taken, and the other left. Ellinor looked out at the vacant deanery with tearful eyes, the last thing at night, the first in the morning. But it is pretty nearly the same with church dignitaries as with kings; the dean is dead, long live the dean! A clergyman from a distant county was appointed, and all the Close was astir to learn and hear every particular connected with him. Luckily he came in at the tag-end of one of the noble families in the peerage; so, at any rate, all his future associates could learn with tolerable certainty that he was forty-two years of age, married, and with eight daughters and one son. The deanery, formerly so quiet and sedate a dwelling of the one old man, was now to be filled with noise and merriment. Iron railings were being placed before three windows, evidently to be the nursery. In the summer publicity of open windows and doors, the sound of the busy carpenters was perpetually heard all over the Close: and by-and-by waggon-loads of furniture and carriage-loads of people began to arrive. Neither Miss Monro nor Ellinor felt themselves of sufficient importance or station to call on the new comers, but they were as well acquainted with the proceedings of the family as if they had been in daily intercourse; they knew that the eldest Miss Beauchamp was seventeen, and very pretty, only one shoulder was higher than the other; that she was dotingly fond of dancing, and talked a great deal in a *tête-à-tête*, but not much if her mamma was by, and never opened her lips at all if the dean was in the room; that the next sister was wonderfully clever, and was supposed to know all the governess could teach her, and to have private lessons in Greek and mathematics from her father; and so on down to the little boy at the preparatory school and the baby-girl in arms. Moreover, Miss Monro, at any rate, could have stood an examination as to the number of servants at the deanery, their division of work, and the hours of their meals. Presently, a very beautiful, haughty-looking young lady made her appearance in the Close, and in the dean's pew. She was said to be his niece, the orphan daughter of his brother, General Beauchamp, come to East Chester to reside for the necessary time before her marriage, which was to be performed in the cathedral by her uncle, the new dignitary. But as callers at the deanery did not see this beautiful bride elect, and as the Beauchamps had not as yet fallen into habits of intimacy with any of their new acquaintances, very little was known of the circumstances of this approaching wedding beyond the particulars given above.

Ellinor and Miss Monro sat at their drawing-room window, a little shaded by the muslin curtains, watching the busy preparations for the marriage, which was to take place the next day. All morning long, hampers of fruit and flowers, boxes from the railway—for by this time East Chester had got a railway—shop messengers, hired assistants, kept passing backwards and forwards in the busy Close. Towards afternoon the bustle subsided, the scaffolding was up, the materials for the next day's feast carried out of sight. It was to be concluded that the bride elect was seeing to the packing of her trousseau, helped by the merry multitude of cousins, and that the servants were arranging the dinner for the day, or the breakfast for the morrow. So Miss Monro had settled it, discussing every detail and every probability as though she were a chief actor, instead of only a distant, uncared-for spectator of the coming event. Ellinor was tired, and now that there was nothing interesting going on, she had fallen back to her sewing, when she was startled by Miss Memo's exclamation:

"Look, look! here are two gentlemen coming along the lime-tree walk! it must be the bridegroom and his friend." Out of much sympathy, and some curiosity, Ellinor bent forward, and saw, just emerging from the shadow of the trees on to the full afternoon sunlit pavement, Mr. Corbet and another gentleman; the former changed, worn, aged, though with still the same fine intellectual face, leaning on the arm of the younger taller man, and talking eagerly. The other gentleman was doubtless the bridegroom, Ellinor said to herself; and yet her prophetic heart did not believe her words. Even before the bright beauty at the deanery looked out of the great oriel window of the drawing-room, and blushed, and smiled, and kissed her hand—a gesture replied to by Mr. Corbet with much *empressement*, while the other man only took off his hat, almost as if he saw her there for the first time—Ellinor's greedy eyes watched him till he was hidden from sight in the deanery, unheeding Miss Monro's eager incoherent sentences, in turn entreating, apologising, comforting, and upbraiding. Then she slowly turned her painful eyes upon Miss Monro's face, and moved her lips without a sound being heard, and fainted dead away. In all her life she had never done so before, and when she came round she was not like herself; in all probability the persistence and wilfulness she, who was usually so meek and docile, showed during the next twenty-four hours, was the consequence of fever. She resolved to be present at the wedding; numbers were going; she would be unseen, unnoticed in the crowd; but whatever befell, go she would, and neither the tears nor the prayers of Miss Monro could keep her back. She gave no reason for this determination; indeed, in all probability she had none to give; so there was no arguing the point. She was inflexible to entreaty, and no one had any authority over her, except, perhaps, distant Mr. Ness. Miss Monro had all sorts of forebodings as to the possible scenes that might come to pass. But all went on as quietly as though the fullest sympathy pervaded every individual of the great numbers assembled. No one guessed that the muffled, veiled figure, sitting in the shadow behind one of the great pillars, was that of one who had once hoped to stand at the altar with the same bridegroom, who now cast tender looks at the beautiful bride; her veil white and fairy-like, Ellinor's black and shrouding as that of any nun.

Already Mr. Corbet's name was known through the country as that of a great lawyer; people discussed his speeches and character far and wide; and the well-informed in legal gossip spoke of him as sure to be offered a judgeship at the next vacancy. So he, though grave, and middle-aged, and somewhat grey, divided attention and remark with his lovely bride, and her pretty train of cousin bridesmaids. Miss Monro need not have feared for Ellinor: she saw and heard all things as in a mist—a dream; as something she had to go through, before she could waken up to a reality of brightness in which her youth, and the hopes of her youth, should be restored, and all these weary years of dreaminess and woe should be revealed as nothing but the nightmare of a night. She sat motionless enough, still enough, Miss Monro by her, watching her as intently as a keeper watches a madman, and with the same purpose—to prevent any outburst even by bodily strength, if such restraint be needed. When all was over; when the principal personages of the ceremony had filed into the vestry to sign their names; when the swarm of townspeople were going out as swiftly as their individual notions of the restraints of the sacred edifice permitted; when the great chords of the "Wedding March" clanged out from the organ, and the loud bells pealed overhead—Ellinor laid her hand in Miss Monro's. "Take me home," she said softly. And Miss Monro led her home as one leads the blind.

CHAPTER XII.

There are some people who imperceptibly float away from their youth into middle age, and thence pass into declining life with the soft and gentle motion of happy years. There are others who are whirled, in spite of themselves, down dizzy rapids of agony away from their youth at one great bound, into old age with another sudden shock; and thence into the vast calm ocean where there are no shore-marks to tell of time.

This last, it seemed, was to be Ellinor's lot. Her youth had gone in a single night, fifteen years ago, and now she appeared to have become an elderly woman; very still and hopeless in look and movement, but as sweet and gentle in speech and smile as ever she had been in her happiest days. All young people, when they came to know her, loved her dearly, though at first they might call her dull, and heavy to get on with; and as for children and old people, her ready watchful sympathy in their joys as well as their sorrows was an unfailing passage to their hearts. After the first great shock of Mr. Corbet's marriage was over, she seemed to pass into a greater peace than she had known for years; the last faint hope of happiness was gone; it would, perhaps, be more accurate to say, of the bright happiness she had planned for herself in her early youth. Unconsciously, she was being weaned from self-seeking in any shape, and her daily life became, if possible, more innocent and pure and holy. One of the canons used to laugh at her for her constant attendance at all the services, and for her devotion to good works, and call her always the reverend sister. Miss Monro was a little annoyed at this faint clerical joke; Ellinor smiled quietly. Miss Monro disapproved of Ellinor's grave ways and sober severe style of dress.

"You may be as good as you like, my dear, and yet go dressed in some pretty colour, instead of those perpetual blacks and greys, and then there would be no need for me to be perpetually telling people you are only four-and-thirty (and they don't believe me, though I tell them so till I am black in the face). Or, if you would but wear a decent-shaped bonnet, instead of always wearing those of the poky shape in fashion when you were seventeen."

The old canon died, and some one was to be appointed in his stead. These clerical preferments and appointments were the all-important interests to the inhabitants of the Close, and the discussion of probabilities came up invariably if any two met together, in street or house, or even in the very cathedral itself. At length it was settled, and announced by the higher powers. An energetic, hard-working clergyman from a distant part of the diocese, Livingstone by name, was to have the vacant canonry.

Miss Monro said that the name was somehow familiar to her, and by degrees she recollected the young curate who had come to inquire after Ellinor in that dreadful illness she had had at Hamley in the year 1829. Ellinor knew nothing of that visit; no more than Miss Monro did of what had passed between the two before that anxious night. Ellinor just thought it possible it might be the same Mr. Livingstone, and would rather it were not, because she did not feel as if she could bear the frequent though not intimate intercourse she must needs have, if such were the case, with one so closely associated with that great time of terror which she was striving to bury out of sight by every effort in her power. Miss Monro, on the contrary, was busy weaving a romance for her pupil; she thought of the passionate interest displayed by the fair young clergyman fifteen years ago, and believed that occasionally men could be constant, and hoped that if Mr. Livingstone were the new canon, he might prove the *rara avis* which exists but once in a century. He came, and it was the same. He looked a little stouter, a little older, but had still the gait and aspect of a young man. His smooth fair face was scarcely lined at all with any marks of care; the blue eyes looked so kindly and peaceful, that Miss Monro could scarcely fancy they were the same which she had seen fast filling with tears; the bland calm look of the whole man needed the ennoblement of his evident devoutness to be raised into the type of holy innocence which some of the Romanists call the "sacerdotal face." His entire soul was in his work, and he looked as little likely to step forth in the character of either a hero of romance or a faithful lover as could be imagined. Still Miss Monro was not discouraged; she remembered the warm, passionate feeling she had once seen break through the calm exterior, and she believed that what had happened once might occur again.

Of course, while all eyes were directed on the new canon, he had to learn who the possessors of those eyes were one by one; and it was probably some time before the idea came into his mind that Miss Wilkins, the lady in black, with the sad pale face, so constant an attendant at service, so regular a visitor at the school, was the same Miss Wilkins as the bright vision of his youth. It was her sweet smile at a painstaking child that betrayed her—if, indeed, betrayal it might be called where there was no wish or effort to conceal anything. Canon Livingstone left the schoolroom almost directly, and, after being for an hour or so in his house, went out to call on Mrs. Randall, the person who knew more of her neighbours' affairs than any one in East Chester.

The next day he called on Miss Wilkins herself. She would have been very glad if he had kept on in his ignorance; it was so keenly painful to be in the company of one the sight of whom, even at a distance, had brought her such a keen remembrance of past misery; and when told of his call, as she was sitting at her sewing in the dining-room, she had to nerve herself for the interview before going upstairs into the drawing-room, where he was being entertained by Miss Monro with warm demonstrations of welcome. A little contraction of the brow, a little compression of the lips, an increased pallor on Ellinor's part, was all that Miss Monro could see in her, though she had put on her glasses with foresight and intention to observe. She turned to the canon; his colour had certainly deepened as he went forwards with out-stretched hand to meet Ellinor. That was all that was to be seen; but on the slight foundation of that blush, Miss Monro built many castles; and when they faded away, one after one, she recognised that they were only baseless visions. She used to put the disappointment of her hopes down to Ellinor's unvaried calmness of demeanour, which might be taken for coldness of disposition; and to her steady refusal to allow Miss Monro to invite Canon Livingstone to the small teas they were in the habit of occasionally giving. Yet he persevered in his calls; about once every fortnight he came, and would sit an hour or more, looking covertly at his watch, as if as Miss Monro shrewdly observed to herself, he did not go away at last because he wished to do so, but because he ought. Sometimes Ellinor was present, sometimes she was away; in this latter case Miss Monro thought she could detect a certain wistful watching of the door every time a noise was heard outside the room. He always avoided any reference to former days at Hamley, and that, Miss Monro feared, was a bad sign.

After this long uniformity of years without any event closely touching on Ellinor's own individual life, with the one great exception of Mr. Corbet's marriage, something happened which much affected her. Mr. Ness died suddenly at his parsonage, and Ellinor learnt it first from Mr. Brown, a clergyman, whose living was near Hamley, and who had been sent for by the Parsonage servants as soon as they discovered that it was not sleep, but death, that made their master so late in rising.

Mr. Brown had been appointed executer by his late friend, and wrote to tell Ellinor that after a few legacies were paid, she was to have a life-interest in the remainder of the small property which Mr. Ness had left, and that it would be necessary for her, as the residuary legatee, to come to Hamley Parsonage as soon as convenient, to decide upon certain courses of action with regard to furniture, books, &c.

Ellinor shrank from this journey, which her love and duty towards her dead friend rendered necessary. She had scarcely left East Chester since she first arrived there, sixteen or seventeen years ago, and she was timorous about the very mode of travelling; and then to go back to Hamley, which she thought never to have seen again! She never spoke much about any feelings of her own, but Miss Monro could always read her silence, and interpreted it into pretty just and forcible words that afternoon when Canon Livingstone called. She liked to talk about Ellinor to him, and suspected that he liked to hear. She was almost annoyed this time by the comfort he would keep giving her; there was no greater danger in travelling by railroad than by coach, a little care about certain things was required, that was all, and the average number of deaths by accidents on railroads was not greater than the average number when people travelled by coach, if you took into consideration the far greater number of travellers. Yes! returning to the deserted scenes of one's youth was very painful ... Had Miss Wilkins made any provision for another lady to take her place as visitor at the school? He believed it was her week. Miss Monro was out of all patience at his entire calmness and reasonableness. Later in the day she became more at peace with him, when she received a kind little note from Mrs. Forbes, a great friend of hers, and the mother of the family she was now teaching, saying that Canon Livingstone had called and told her that Ellinor had to go on a very painful journey, and that Mrs. Forbes was quite sure Miss Monro's companionship upon it would be a great comfort to both, and that she could perfectly be set at liberty for a fortnight or so, for it would fall in admirably with the fact that "Jeanie was growing tall, and the doctor had advised sea air this spring; so a month's holiday would suit them now even better than later on." Was this going straight to Mrs. Forbes, to whom she should herself scarcely have liked to name it, the act of a good, thoughtful man, or of a lover? questioned Miss Monro; but she could not answer her own inquiry, and had to be very grateful for the deed, without accounting for the motives.

A coach met the train at a station about ten miles from Hamley, and Dixon was at the inn where the coach stopped, ready to receive them.

The old man was almost in tears at the sight of them again in a familiar place. He had put on his Sunday clothes to do them honour; and to conceal his agitation he kept up a pretended bustle about their luggage. To the indignation of the inn-porters, who were of a later generation, he would wheel it himself to the Parsonage, though he broke down from fatigue once or twice on the way, and had to stand and rest, his ladies waiting by his side, and making remarks on the alterations of houses and the places of trees, in order to give him ample time to recruit himself, for there was no one to wait for them and give them a welcome to the Parsonage, which was to be their temporary home. The respectful servants, in deep mourning, had all prepared, and gave Ellinor a note from Mr. Brown, saying that he purposely refrained from disturbing them that day after their long journey, but would call on the morrow, and tell them of the arrangements he had thought of making, always subject to Miss Wilkins's approval.

These were simple enough; certain legal forms to be gone through, any selection from books or furniture to be made, and the rest to be sold by auction as speedily as convenient, as the successor to the living might wish to have repairs and alterations effected in the old parsonage. For some days Ellinor employed herself in business in the house, never going out except to church. Miss Monro, on the contrary, strolled about everywhere, noticing all the alterations in place and people, which were never improvements in her opinion. Ellinor had plenty of callers (her tenants, Mr. and Mrs. Osbaldistone among others), but, excepting in rare cases—most of them belonged to humble life—she declined to see every one, as she had business enough on her hands: sixteen years makes a great difference in any set of people. The old acquaintances of her father in his better days were almost all dead or removed; there were one or two remaining, and these Ellinor received; one or two more, old and infirm, confined to their houses, she planned to call upon before leaving Hamley. Every evening, when Dixon had done his work at Mr. Osbaldistone's, he came up to the Parsonage, ostensibly to help her in moving or packing books, but really because these two clung to each other—were bound to each other by a bond never to be spoken about. It was understood between them that once before Ellinor left she should go and see the old place, Ford Bank. Not to go into the house, though Mr. and Mrs. Osbaldistone had begged her to name her own time for revisiting it when they and their family would be absent, but to see all the gardens and grounds once more; a solemn, miserable visit, which, because of the very misery it involved, appeared to Ellinor to be an imperative duty.

Dixon and she talked together as she sat making a catalogue one evening in the old low-browed library; the casement windows were open into the garden, and the May showers had brought out the scents of the new-leaved sweetbriar bush just below. Beyond the garden hedge the grassy meadows sloped away down to the liver; the Parsonage was so much raised that, sitting in the house, you could see over the boundary hedge. Men with instruments were busy in the meadow. Ellinor, pausing in her work, asked Dixon what they were doing.

"Them's the people for the new railway," said he. "Nought would satisfy the Hamley folk but to have a railway all to themselves—coaches isn't good enough now-a-days."

He spoke with a tone of personal offence natural to a man who had passed all his life among horses, and considered railway-engines as their despicable rivals, conquering only by stratagem.

By-and-by Ellinor passed on to a subject the consideration of which she had repeatedly urged upon Dixon, and entreated him to come and form one of their household at East Chester. He was growing old, she thought older even in looks and feelings than in years, and she would make him happy and comfortable in his declining years if he would but come and pass them under her care. The addition which Mr. Ness's bequest made to her income would enable her to do not only this, but to relieve Miss Monro of her occupation of teaching; which, at the years she had arrived at, was becoming burdensome. When she proposed the removal to Dixon he shook his head.

"It's not that I don't thank you, and kindly, too; but I'm too old to go chopping and changing."

"But it would be no change to come back to me, Dixon," said Ellinor.

"Yes, it would. I were born i' Hamley, and it's i' Hamley I reckon to die."

On her urging him a little more, it came out that he had a strong feeling that if he did not watch the spot where the dead man lay buried, the whole would be discovered; and that this dread of his had often poisoned the pleasure of his visit to East Chester.

"I don't rightly know how it is, for I sometimes think if it wasn't for you, missy, I should be glad to have made it all clear before I go; and yet at times I dream, or it comes into my head as I lie awake with the rheumatics, that some one is there, digging; or that I hear 'em cutting down the tree; and then I get up and look out of the loft window—you'll mind the window over the stables, as looks into the garden, all covered over wi' the leaves of the jargonelle pear-tree? That were my room when first I come as stable-boy, and tho' Mr. Osbaldistone would fain give me a warmer one, I allays tell him I like th' old place best. And by times I've getten up five or six times a-night to make sure as there was no one at work under the tree."

Ellinor shivered a little. He saw it, and restrained himself in the relief he was receiving from imparting his superstitious fancies.

"You see, missy, I could never rest a-nights if I didn't feel as if I kept the secret in my hand, and held it tight day and night, so as I could open my hand at any minute and see as it was there. No! my own little missy will let me come and see her now and again, and I know as I can allays ask her for what I want: and if it please God to lay me by, I shall tell her so, and she'll see as I want for nothing. But somehow I could ne'er bear leaving Hamley. You shall come and follow me to my grave when my time comes."

"Don't talk so, please, Dixon," said she.

"Nay, it'll be a mercy when I can lay me down and sleep in peace: though I sometimes fear as peace will not come to me even there." He was going out of the room, and was now more talking to himself than to her. "They say blood will out, and if it weren't for her part in it, I could wish for a clear breast before I die."

She did not hear the latter part of this mumbled sentence. She was looking at a letter just brought in and requiring an immediate answer. It was from Mr. Brown. Notes from him were of daily occurrence, but this contained an open letter the writing of which was strangely familiar to her—it did not need the signature "Ralph Corbet," to tell her whom the letter came from. For some moments she could not read the words. They expressed a simple enough request, and were addressed to the auctioneer who was to dispose of the rather valuable library of the late Mr. Ness, and whose name had been advertised in connection with the sale, in the *Athenæum*, and other similar papers. To him Mr. Corbet wrote, saying that he should be unable to be present when the books were sold, but that he wished to be allowed to buy in, at any price decided upon, a certain rare folio edition of *Virgil*, bound in parchment, and with notes in Italian. The book was fully described. Though no Latin scholar, Ellinor knew the book well—remembered its look from old times, and could instantly have laid her hand upon it. The auctioneer had sent the request onto his employer, Mr. Brown. That gentleman applied to Ellinor for her consent. She saw that the fact of the intended sale must be all that Mr. Corbet was aware of, and that he could not know to whom the books belonged. She chose out the book, and wrapped and tied it up with trembling hands. *He* might be the person to untie the knot. It was strangely familiar to her love, after so many years, to be brought into thus much contact with him. She wrote a short note to Mr. Brown, in which she requested him to say, as though from himself; and without any mention of her name, that he, as executor, requested Mr. Corbet's acceptance of the *Virgil*, as a remembrance of his former friend and tutor. Then she rang the bell, and gave the letter and parcel to the servant.

Again alone, and Mr. Corbet's open letter on the table. She took it up and looked at it till the letters dazzled crimson on the white paper. Her life rolled backwards, and she was a girl again. At last she roused herself; but instead of destroying the note—it was long years since all her love-letters from him had been returned to the writer—she unlocked her little writing-case again, and placed this letter carefully down at the bottom, among the dead rose-leaves which embalmed the note from her father, found after his death under his pillow, the little golden curl of her sister's, the half-finished sewing of her mother.

The shabby writing-case itself was given her by her father long ago, and had since been taken with her everywhere. To be sure, her changes of place had been but few; but if she had gone to Nova Zembla, the sight of that little leather box on awaking from her first sleep, would have given her a sense of home. She locked the case up again, and felt all the richer for that morning.

A day or two afterwards she left Hamley. Before she went she compelled herself to go round the gardens and grounds of Ford Bank. She had made Mrs. Osbaldistone understand that it would be painful for her to re-enter the house; but Mr. Osbaldistone accompanied her in her walk.

"You see how literally we have obeyed the clause in the lease which ties us out from any alterations," said he, smiling. "We are living in a tangled thicket of wood. I must confess that I should have liked to cut down a good deal; but we do not do even the requisite thinnings without making the proper application for leave to

Mr. Johnson. In fact, your old friend Dixon is jealous of every pea-stick the gardener cuts. I never met with so faithful a fellow. A good enough servant, too, in his way; but somewhat too old-fashioned for my wife and daughters, who complain of his being surly now and then."

"You are not thinking of parting with him?" said Ellinor, jealous for Dixon.

"Oh, no; he and I are capital friends. And I believe Mrs. Osbaldistone herself would never consent to his leaving us. But some ladies, you know, like a little more subserviency in manner than our friend Dixon can boast."

Ellinor made no reply. They were entering the painted flower garden, hiding the ghastly memory. She could not speak. She felt as if, with all her striving, she could not move—just as one does in a nightmare—but she was past the place even as this terror came to its acme; and when she came to herself, Mr. Osbaldistone was still blandly talking, and saying—

"It is now a reward for our obedience to your wishes, Miss Wilkins, for if the projected railway passes through the ash-field yonder we should have been perpetually troubled with the sight of the trains; indeed, the sound would have been much more distinct than it will be now coming through the interlacing branches. Then you will not go in, Miss Wilkins?" Mrs. Osbaldistone desired me to say how happy—"Ah! I can understand such feelings—Certainly, certainly; it is so much the shortest way to the town, that we elder ones always go through the stable-yard; for young people, it is perhaps not quite so desirable. Ha! Dixon," he continued, "on the watch for the Miss Ellinor we so often hear of! This old man," he continued to Ellinor, "is never satisfied with the seat of our young ladies, always comparing their way of riding with that of a certain missy—"

"I cannot help it, sir; they've quite a different style of hand, and sit all lumpish-like. Now, Miss Ellinor, there—"

"Hush, Dixon," she said, suddenly aware of why the old servant was not popular with his mistress. "I suppose I may be allowed to ask for Dixon's company for an hour or so; we have something to do together before we leave."

The consent given, the two walked away, as by previous appointment, to Hamley churchyard, where he was to point out to her the exact spot where he wished to be buried. Trampling over the long, rank grass, but avoiding passing directly over any of the thickly-strewn graves, he made straight for one spot—a little space of unoccupied ground close by, where Molly, the pretty scullery-maid, lay:

Sacred to the Memory of
MARY GREAVES.
Born 1797. Died 1818.
"We part to meet again."

"I put this stone up over her with my first savings," said he, looking at it; and then, pulling out his knife, he began to clean out the letters. "I said then as I would lie by her. And it'll be a comfort to think you'll see me laid here. I trust no one'll be so crabbed as to take a fancy to this 'ere spot of ground."

Ellinor grasped eagerly at the only pleasure which her money enabled her to give to the old man: and promised him that she would take care and buy the right to that particular piece of ground. This was evidently a gratification Dixon had frequently yearned after; he kept saying, "I'm greatly obleeged to ye, Miss Ellinor. I may say I'm truly obleeged." And when he saw them off by the coach the next day, his last words were, "I cannot justly say how greatly I'm obleeged to you for that matter of the churchyard." It was a much more easy affair to give Miss Monro some additional comforts; she was as cheerful as ever; still working away at her languages in any spare time, but confessing that she was tired of the perpetual teaching in which her life had been spent during the last thirty years. Ellinor was now enabled to set her at liberty from this, and she accepted the kindness from her former pupil with as much simple gratitude as that with which a mother receives a favour from a child. "If Ellinor were but married to Canon Livingstone, I should be happier than I have ever been since my father died," she used to say to herself in the solitude of her bed-chamber, for talking aloud had become her wont in the early years of her isolated life as a governess. "And yet," she went on, "I don't know what I should do without her; it is lucky for me that things are not in my hands, for a pretty mess I should make of them, one way or another. Dear! how old Mrs. Cadogan used to hate that word 'mess,' and correct her granddaughters for using it right before my face, when I knew I had said it myself only the moment before! Well! those days are all over now. God be thanked!"

In spite of being glad that "things were not in her hands" Miss Monro tried to take affairs into her charge by doing all she could to persuade Ellinor to allow her to invite the canon to their "little sociable teas." The most provoking part was, that she was sure he would have come if he had been asked; but she could never get leave to do so. "Of course no man could go on for ever and ever without encouragement," as she confided to herself in a plaintive tone of voice; and by-and-by many people were led to suppose that the bachelor canon was paying attention to Miss Forbes, the eldest daughter of the family to which the delicate Jeanie belonged. It was, perhaps, with the Forbeses that both Miss Monro and Ellinor were the most intimate of all the families in East Chester. Mrs. Forbes was a widow lady of good means, with a large family of pretty, delicate daughters. She herself belonged to one of the great houses in ---shire, but had married into Scotland; so, after her husband's death, it was the most natural thing in the world that she should settle in East Chester; and one after another of her daughters had become first Miss Monro's pupil and afterwards her friend. Mrs. Forbes herself had always been strongly attracted by Ellinor, but it was long before she could conquer the timid reserve by which Miss Wilkins was hedged round. It was Miss Monro, who was herself incapable of jealousy, who persevered in praising them to one another, and in bringing them together; and now Ellinor was as intimate and familiar in Mrs. Forbes's household as she ever could be with any family not her own.

Mrs. Forbes was considered to be a little fanciful as to illness; but it was no wonder, remembering how many sisters she had lost by consumption. Miss Monro had often grumbled at the way in which her pupils were made irregular for very trifling causes. But no one so alarmed as she, when, in the autumn succeeding Mr. Ness's death, Mrs. Forbes remarked to her on Ellinor's increased delicacy of appearance, and shortness of breathing. From that time forwards she worried Ellinor (if any one so sweet and patient could ever have been worried) with respirators and precautions. Ellinor submitted to all her friend's wishes and cares, sooner than make her anxious, and remained a prisoner in the house through the whole of November. Then Miss Monro's anxiety took another turn. Ellinor's appetite and spirits failed her—not at all an unnatural consequence of so many weeks' confinement to the house. A plan was started, quite suddenly, one morning in December, that met with approval from everyone but Ellinor, who was, however, by this time too languid to make much resistance.

Mrs. Forbes and her daughters were going to Rome for three or four months, so as to avoid the trying east winds of spring; why should not Miss Wilkins go with them? They urged it, and Miss Monro urged it, though with a little private sinking of the heart at the idea of the long separation from one who was almost like a child to her. Ellinor was, as it were, lifted off her feet and borne away by the unanimous opinion of others—the doctor included—who decided that such a step was highly desirable; if not absolutely necessary. She knew that she had only a life interest both in her father's property and in that bequeathed to her by Mr. Ness. Hitherto she had not felt much troubled by this, as she had supposed that in the natural course of events she should survive Miss Monro and Dixon, both of whom she looked upon as dependent upon her. All she had to bequeath to the two was the small savings, which would not nearly suffice for both purposes, especially considering that Miss Monro had given up her teaching, and that both she and Dixon were passing into years.

Before Ellinor left England she had made every arrangement for the contingency of her death abroad that Mr. Johnson could suggest. She had written and sent a long letter to Dixon; and a shorter one was left in charge of Canon Livingstone (she dared not hint at the possibility of her dying to Miss Monro) to be sent to the old man.

As they drove out of the King's Cross station, they passed a gentleman's carriage entering. Ellinor saw a bright, handsome lady, a nurse, and baby inside, and a gentleman sitting by them whose face she could never forget. It was Mr. Corbet taking his wife and child to the railway. They were going on a Christmas visit to East Chester deanery. He had been leaning back, not noticing the passers-by, not attending to the other inmates of the carriage, probably absorbed in the consideration of some law case. Such were the casual glimpses Ellinor had of one with whose life she had once thought herself bound up.

Who so proud as Miss Monro when a foreign letter came? Her correspondent was not particularly graphic in her descriptions, nor were there any adventures to be described, nor was the habit of mind of Ellinor such as to make her clear and definite in her own impressions of what she saw, and her natural reserve kept her from being fluent in communicating them even to Miss Monro. But that lady would have been pleased to read aloud these letters to the assembled dean and canons, and would not have been surprised if they had invited her to the chapter-house for that purpose. To her circle of untravelled ladies, ignorant of Murray, but laudably desirous of information, all Ellinor's historical reminiscences and rather formal details were really interesting. There was no railroad in those days between Lyons and Marseilles, so their progress was slow, and the passage of letters to and fro, when they had arrived in Rome, long and uncertain. But all seemed going on well. Ellinor spoke of herself as in better health; and Canon Livingstone (between whom and Miss Monro great intimacy had sprung up since Ellinor had gone away, and Miss Monro could ask him to tea) confirmed this report of Miss Wilkins's health from a letter which he had received from Mrs. Forbes. Curiosity about that letter was Miss Monro's torment. What could they have had to write to each other about? It was a very odd proceeding; although the Livingstones and Forbeses were distantly related, after the manner of Scotland. Could it have been that he had offered to Euphemia, after all, and that her mother had answered; or, possibly, there was a letter from Effie herself, enclosed. It was a pity for Miss Monro's peace of mind that she did not ask him straight away. She would then have learnt what Canon Livingstone had no thought of concealing, that Mrs. Forbes had written solely to give him some fuller directions about certain charities than she had had time to think about in the hurry of starting. As it was, and when, a little later on, she heard him speak of the possibility of his going himself to Rome, as soon as his term of residence was over, in time for the Carnival, she gave up her fond project in despair, and felt very much like a child whose house of bricks had been knocked down by the unlucky waft of some passing petticoat.

Meanwhile, the entire change of scene brought on the exquisite refreshment of entire change of thought. Ellinor had not been able so completely to forget her past life for many years; it was like a renewing of her youth; cut so suddenly short by the shears of Fate. Ever since that night, she had had to rouse herself on awakening in the morning into a full comprehension of the great cause she had for much fear and heavy grief. Now, when she wakened in her little room, fourth piano, No. 36, Babuino, she saw the strange, pretty things around her, and her mind went off into pleasant wonder and conjecture, happy recollections of the day before, and pleasant anticipations of the day to come. Latent in Ellinor was her father's artistic temperament; everything new and strange was a picture and a delight; the merest group in the street, a Roman facchino, with his cloak draped over his shoulder, a girl going to market or carrying her pitcher back from the fountain, everything and every person that presented it or himself to her senses, gave them a delicious shock, as if it were something strangely familiar from Pinelli, but unseen by her mortal eyes before. She forgot her despondency, her ill-health disappeared as if by magic; the Misses Forbes, who had taken the pensive, drooping invalid as a companion out of kindness of heart, found themselves amply rewarded by the sight of her amended health, and her keen enjoyment of everything, and the half-quaint, half naive expressions of her pleasure.

So March came round; Lent was late that year. The great nosegays of violets and camellias were for sale at the corner of the Condotti, and the revellers had no difficulty in procuring much rarer flowers for the belles of the Corso. The embassies had their balconies; the attachés of the Russian Embassy threw their light and lovely presents at every pretty girl, or suspicion of a pretty girl, who passed slowly in her carriage, covered over with her white domino, and holding her wire mask as a protection to her face from the showers of lime confetti, which otherwise would have been enough to blind her; Mrs. Forbes had her own hired balcony, as became a wealthy and respectable Englishwoman. The girls had a great basket full of bouquets with which to pelt their friends in the crowd below; a store of moccoletti lay piled on the table behind, for it was the last day of Carnival, and as soon as dusk came on the tapers were to be lighted, to be as quickly extinguished by every means in everyone's power. The crowd below was at its wildest pitch; the rows of stately contadini alone sitting immovable as their possible ancestors, the senators who received Brennus and his Gauls. Masks and white dominoes, foreign gentlemen, and the riffraff of the city, slow-driving carriages, showers of flowers, most of them faded by this time, everyone shouting and struggling at that wild pitch of excitement which may so soon turn into fury. The Forbes girls had given place at the window to their mother and Ellinor, who were gazing half amused, half terrified, at the mad parti-coloured movement below; when a familiar face looked up, smiling a recognition; and "How shall I get to you?" was asked in English, by the well-known voice of Canon Livingstone. They saw him disappear under the balcony on which they were standing, but it was some time before he made his appearance in their room. And when he did, he was almost overpowered with greetings; so glad were they to see an East Chester face.

"When did you come? Where are you? What a pity you did not come sooner! It is so long since we have heard anything; do tell us everything! It is three weeks since we have had any letters; those tiresome boats have been so irregular because of the weather." "How was everybody—Miss Monro in particular?" Ellinor asks.

He, quietly smiling, replied to their questions by slow degrees. He had only arrived the night before, and had been hunting for them all day; but no one could give him any distinct intelligence as to their whereabouts in all the noise and confusion of the place, especially as they had their only English servant with them, and the canon was not strong in his Italian. He was not sorry he had missed all but this last day of carnival, for he was half blinded and wholly deafened, as it was. He was at the "Angleterre;" he had left East Chester about a week ago; he had letters for all of them, but had not dared to bring them through the crowd for fear of having his pocket picked. Miss Monro was very well, but very uneasy at not having heard from Ellinor for so long; the irregularity of the boats must be telling both ways, for their English friends were full of wonder at not hearing from Rome. And then followed some well-deserved abuse of the Roman post, and some suspicion of the carelessness with which Italian servants posted English letters. All these answers were satisfactory enough, yet Mrs. Forbes thought she saw a latent uneasiness in Canon Livingstone's manner, and fancied once or twice that he hesitated in replying to Ellinor's questions. But there was no being quite sure in the increasing darkness, which prevented countenances from being seen; nor in the constant interruptions and screams which were going on in the small crowded room, as wafting handkerchiefs, puffs of wind, or veritable extinguishers, fastened to long sticks, and coming from nobody knew where, put out taper after taper as fast as they were lighted.

"You will come home with us," said Mrs. Forbes. "I can only offer you cold meat with tea; our cook is gone out, this being a universal festa; but we cannot part with an old friend for any scruples as to the commissariat."

"Thank you. I should have invited myself if you had not been good enough to ask me."

When they had all arrived at their apartment in the Babuino (Canon Livingstone had gone round to fetch the letters with which he was entrusted), Mrs. Forbes was confirmed in her supposition that he had something particular and not very pleasant to say to Ellinor, by the rather grave and absent manner in which he awaited her return from taking off her out-of-door things. He broke off, indeed, in his conversation with Mrs. Forbes to go and meet Ellinor, and to lead her into the most distant window before he delivered her letters.

"From what you said in the balcony yonder, I fear you have not received your home letters regularly?"

"No!" replied she, startled and trembling, she hardly knew why.

"No more has Miss Monro heard from you; nor, I believe, has some one else who expected to hear. Your man of business—I forget his name."

"My man of business! Something has gone wrong, Mr. Livingstone. Tell me—I want to know. I have been expecting it—only tell me." She sat down suddenly, as white as ashes.

"Dear Miss Wilkins, I'm afraid it is painful enough, but you are fancying it worse than it is. All your friends are quite well; but an old servant—"

"Well!" she said, seeing his hesitation, and leaning forwards and griping at his arm.

"Is taken up on a charge of manslaughter or murder. Oh! Mrs. Forbes, come here!"

For Ellinor had fainted, falling forwards on the arm she had held. When she came round she was lying half undressed on her bed; they were giving her tea in spoonfuls.

"I must get up," she moaned. "I must go home."

"You must lie still," said Mrs. Forbes, firmly.

"You don't know. I must go home," she repeated; and she tried to sit up, but fell back helpless. Then she did not speak, but lay and thought. "Will you bring me some meat?" she whispered. "And some wine?" They brought her meat and wine; she ate, though she was choking. "Now, please, bring me my letters, and leave me alone; and after that I should like to speak to Canon Livingstone. Don't let him go, please. I won't be long—half an hour, I think. Only let me be alone."

There was a hurried feverish sharpness in her tone that made Mrs. Forbes very anxious, but she judged it best to comply with her requests.

The letters were brought, the lights were arranged so that she could read them lying on her bed; and they left her. Then she got up and stood on her feet, dizzy enough, her arms clasped at the top of her head, her eyes dilated and staring as if looking at some great horror. But after a few minutes she sat down suddenly, and began to read. Letters were evidently missing. Some had been sent by an opportunity that had been delayed on the journey, and had not yet arrived in Rome. Others had been despatched by the post, but the severe weather, the unusual snow, had, in those days, before the railway was made between Lyons and Marseilles, put a stop to many a traveller's plans, and had rendered the transmission of the mail extremely uncertain; so, much of that intelligence which Miss Monro had evidently considered as certain to be known to Ellinor was entirely matter of conjecture, and could only be guessed at from what was told in these letters. One was from Mr. Johnson, one from Mr. Brown, one from Miss Monro; of course the last mentioned was the first read. She spoke of the shock of the discovery of Mr. Dunster's body, found in the cutting of the new line of railroad from Hamley to the nearest railway station; the body so hastily buried long ago, in its clothes, by which it was now recognised—a recognition confirmed by one or two more personal and indestructible things, such as his watch and seal with his initials; of the shock to everyone, the Osbaldistones in particular, on the further discovery of a fleam or horse-lancet, having the name of Abraham Dixon engraved on the handle; how Dixon had gone on Mr. Osbaldistone's business to a horse-fair in Ireland some weeks before this, and had had his leg broken by a kick from an unruly mare, so that he was barely able to move about when the officers of justice went to apprehend him in Tralee.

At this point Ellinor cried out loud and shrill.

"Oh, Dixon! Dixon! and I was away enjoying myself."

They heard her cry, and came to the door, but it was bolted inside.

"Please, go away," she said; "please, go. I will be very quiet; only, please, go."

She could not bear just then to read any more of Miss Monro's letter; she tore open Mr. Johnson's—the date was a fortnight earlier than Miss Monro's; he also expressed his wonder at not hearing from her, in reply to his letter of January 9; but he added, that he thought that her trustees had judged rightly; the handsome sum the railway company had offered for the land when their surveyor decided on the alteration of the line, Mr. Osbaldistone, &c. &c. She could not read anymore; it was Fate pursuing her. Then she took the letter up again and tried to read; but all that reached her understanding was the fact that Mr. Johnson had sent his present letter to Miss Monro, thinking that she might know of some private opportunity safer than the post. Mr. Brown's was just such a letter as he occasionally sent her from time to time; a correspondence that arose out of their mutual regard for their dead friend Mr. Ness. It, too, had been sent to Miss Monro to direct. Ellinor was on the point of putting it aside entirely, when the name of Corbet caught her eye: "You will be interested to hear that the old pupil of our departed friend, who was so anxious to obtain the folio *Virgil* with the Italian notes, is appointed the new judge in room of Mr. Justice Jenkin. At least I conclude that Mr. Ralph Corbet, Q.C., is the same as the *Virgil* fancier."

"Yes," said Ellinor, bitterly; "he judged well; it would never have done." They were the first words of anything like reproach which she ever formed in her own mind during all these years. She thought for a few moments of the old times; it seemed to steady her brain to think of them. Then she took up and finished Miss Monro's letter. That excellent friend had done all which she thought Ellinor would have wished without delay. She had written to Mr. Johnson, and charged him to do everything he could to defend Dixon and to spare no expense. She was thinking of going to the prison in the county town, to see the old man herself, but Ellinor could perceive that all these endeavours and purposes of Miss Monro's were based on love for her own pupil, and a desire to set her mind at ease as far as she could, rather than from any idea that Dixon himself could be innocent. Ellinor put down the letters, and went to the door, then turned back, and locked them up in her writing-case with trembling hands; and after that she entered the drawing-room, looking liker to a ghost than to a living woman.

"Can I speak to you for a minute alone?" Her still, tuneless voice made the words into a command. Canon Livingstone arose and followed her into the little dining-room. "Will you tell me all you know—all you have heard about my—you know what?"

"Miss Monro was my informant—at least at first—it was in the *Times* the day before I left. Miss Monro says it could only have been done in a moment of anger if the old servant is really guilty; that he was as steady and good a man as she ever knew, and she seems to have a strong feeling against Mr. Dunster, as always giving your father much unnecessary trouble; in fact, she hints that his disappearance at the time was supposed to be the cause of a considerable loss of property to Mr. Wilkins."

"No!" said Ellinor, eagerly, feeling that some justice ought to be done to the dead man; and then she stopped short, fearful of saying anything that should betray her full knowledge. "I mean this," she went on; "Mr. Dunster was a very disagreeable man personally—and papa—we none of us liked him; but he was quite honest—please remember that."

The canon bowed, and said a few acquiescing words. He waited for her to speak again.

"Miss Monro says she is going to see Dixon in—"

"Oh, Mr. Livingstone, I can't bear it!"

He let her alone, looking at her pitifully, as she twisted and wrung her hands together in her endeavour to regain the quiet manner she had striven to maintain through the interview. She looked up at him with a poor attempt at an apologetic smile:

"It is so terrible to think of that good old man in prison!"

"You do not believe him guilty!" said Canon Livingstone, in some surprise. "I am afraid, from all I heard and read, there is but little doubt that he did kill the man; I trust in some moment of irritation, with no premeditated malice."

Ellinor shook her head.

"How soon can I get to England?" asked she. "I must start at once."

"Mrs. Forbes sent out while you were lying down. I am afraid there is no boat to Marseilles till Thursday, the day after to-morrow."

"But I must go sooner!" said Ellinor, starting up. "I must go; please help me. He may be tried before I can get there!"

"Alas! I fear that will be the case, whatever haste you make. The trial was to come on at the Hellingford Assizes, and that town stands first on the Midland Circuit list. To-day is the 27th of February; the assizes begin on the 7th of March."

"I will start to-morrow morning early for Civita; there may be a boat there they do not know of here. At any rate, I shall be on my way. If he dies, I must die too. Oh! I don't know what I am saying, I am so utterly crushed down! It would be such a kindness if you would go away, and let no one come to me. I know Mrs. Forbes is so good, she will forgive me. I will say good-by to you all before I go to-morrow morning; but I must think now."

For one moment he stood looking at her as if he longed to comfort her by more words. He thought better of it, however, and silently left the room.

For a long time Ellinor sat still; now and then taking up Miss Monro's letter, and re-reading the few terrible details. Then she bethought her that possibly the canon might have brought a copy of the *Times*, containing the examination of Dixon before the magistrates, and she opened the door and called to a passing servant to make the inquiry. She was quite right in her conjecture; Dr. Livingstone had had the paper in his pocket during his interview with her; but he thought the evidence so conclusive, that the perusal of it would only be adding to her extreme distress by accelerating the conviction of Dixon's guilt, which he believed she must arrive at sooner or later.

He had been reading the report over with Mrs. Forbes and her daughters, after his return from Ellinor's room, and they were all participating in his opinion upon it, when her request for the *Times* was brought. They had reluctantly agreed, saying there did not appear to be a shadow of doubt on the fact of Dixon's having killed Mr. Dunster, only hoping there might prove to be some extenuating circumstances, which Ellinor had probably recollected, and which she was desirous of producing on the approaching trial.

CHAPTER XIII.

Ellinor, having read the report of Dixon's examination in the newspaper, bathed her eyes and forehead in cold water, and tried to still her poor heart's beating, that she might be clear and collected enough to weigh the evidence.

Every line of it was condemnatory. One or two witnesses spoke of Dixon's unconcealed dislike of Dunster, a dislike which Ellinor knew had been entertained by the old servant out of a species of loyalty to his master, as well as from personal distaste. The fleam was proved beyond all doubt to be Dixon's; and a man, who had been stable-boy in Mr. Wilkins's service, swore that on the day when Mr. Dunster was missed, and when the whole town was wondering what had become of him, a certain colt of Mr. Wilkins's had needed bleeding, and that he had been sent by Dixon to the farrier's for a horse-lancet, an errand which he had remarked upon at the time, as he knew that Dixon had a fleam of his own.

Mr. Osbaldistone was examined. He kept interrupting himself perpetually to express his surprise at the fact of so steady and well-conducted a man as Dixon being guilty of so heinous a crime, and was willing enough to testify to the excellent character which he had borne during all the many years he had been in his (Mr. Osbaldistone's) service; but he appeared to be quite convinced by the evidence previously given of the prisoner's guilt in the matter, and strengthened the case against him materially by stating the circumstance of the old man's dogged unwillingness to have the slightest interference by cultivation with that particular piece of ground.

Here Ellinor shuddered. Before her, in that Roman bed-chamber, rose the fatal oblong she knew by heart—a little green moss or lichen, and thinly-growing blades of grass scarcely covering the caked and undisturbed soil under the old tree. Oh, that she had been in England when the surveyors of the railway between Ashcombe and Hamley had altered their line; she would have entreated, implored, compelled her trustees not to have sold that piece of ground for any sum of money whatever. She would have bribed the surveyors, done she knew not what—but now it was too late; she would not let her mind wander off to what might have been; she would force herself again to attend to the newspaper columns. There was little more: the prisoner had been asked if he could say anything to clear himself, and properly cautioned not to say anything to incriminate himself. The poor old man's person was described, and his evident emotion. "The prisoner was observed to clutch at the rail before him to steady himself, and his colour changed so much at this part of the evidence that one of the turnkeys offered him a glass of water, which he declined. He is a man of a strongly-built frame, and with rather a morose and sullen cast of countenance."

"My poor, poor Dixon!" said Ellinor, laying down the paper for an instant, and she was near crying, only she had resolved to shed no tears till she had finished all, and could judge of the chances. There were but a few lines more: "At one time the prisoner seemed to be desirous of alleging something in his defence, but he changed his mind, if such had been the case, and in reply to Mr. Gordon (the magistrate) he only said, 'You've made a pretty strong case out again me, gentlemen, and it seems for to satisfy you; so I think I'll not disturb your minds by saying anything more.' Accordingly, Dixon now stands committed for trial for murder at the next Hellingford Assizes, which commence on March the seventh, before Baron Rushton and Mr. Justice Corbet."

"Mr. Justice Corbet!" The words ran through Ellinor as though she had been stabbed with a knife, and by an irrepressible movement she stood up rigid. The young man, her lover in her youth, the old servant who in those days was perpetually about her—the two who had so often met in familiar if not friendly relations, now to face each other as judge and accused! She could not tell how much Mr. Corbet had conjectured from the partial revelation she had made to him of the impending shame that hung over her and hers. A day or two ago she could have remembered the exact words she had used in that memorable interview; but now, strive as she would, she could only recall facts, not words. After all, the Mr. Justice Corbet might not be Ralph. There was one chance in a hundred against the identity of the two.

While she was weighing probabilities in her sick dizzy mind, she heard soft steps outside her bolted door, and low voices whispering. It was the bedtime of happy people with hearts at ease. Some of the footsteps passed lightly on; but there was a gentle rap at Ellinor's door. She pressed her two hot hands hard against her temples for an instant before she went to open the door. There stood Mrs. Forbes in her handsome evening dress, holding a lighted lamp in her hand.

"May I come in, my dear?" she asked. Ellinor's stiff dry lips refused to utter the words of assent which indeed did not come readily from her heart.

"I am so grieved at this sad news which the canon brings. I can well understand what a shock it must be to you; we have just been saying it must be as bad for you as it would be to us if our old Donald should turn out to have been a hidden murderer all these years that he has lived with us; I really could have as soon suspected Donald as that white-haired respectable old man who used to come and see you at East Chester."

Ellinor felt that she must say something. "It is a terrible shock—poor old man! and no friend near him, even Mr. Osbaldistone giving evidence again him. Oh, dear, dear! why did I ever come to Rome?"

"Now, my dear, you must not let yourself take an exaggerated view of the case. Sad and shocking as it is to have been so deceived, it is what happens to many of us, though not to so terrible a degree; and as to your coming to Rome having anything to do with it—"

(Mrs. Forbes almost smiled at the idea, so anxious was she to banish the idea of self-reproach from Ellinor's sensitive mind, but Ellinor interrupted her abruptly:)

"Mrs. Forbes! did he—did Canon Livingstone tell you that I must leave to-morrow? I must go to England as fast as possible to do what I can for Dixon."

"Yes, he told us you were thinking of it, and it was partly that made me force myself in upon you to-night. I think, my love, you are mistaken in feeling as if you were called upon to do more than what the canon tells me Miss Monro has already done in your name—engaged the best legal advice, and spared no expense to give the suspected man every chance. What could you do more even if you were on the spot? And it is very possible that the trial may have come on before you get home. Then what could you do? He would either have been acquitted or condemned; if the former, he would find public sympathy all in his favour; it always is for the unjustly accused. And if he turns out to be guilty, my dear Ellinor, it will be far better for you to have all the softening which distance can give to such a dreadful termination to the life of a poor man whom you have respected so long."

But Ellinor spoke again with a kind of irritated determination, very foreign to her usual soft docility:

"Please just let me judge for myself this once. I am not ungrateful. God knows I don't want to vex one who has been so kind to me as you have been, dear Mrs. Forbes; but I must go—and every word you say to dissuade me only makes me more convinced. I am going to Civita to-morrow. I shall be that much on the way. I cannot rest here."

Mrs. Forbes looked at her in grave silence. Ellinor could not bear the consciousness of that fixed gaze. Yet its fixity only arose from Mrs. Forbes' perplexity as to how best to assist Ellinor, whether to restrain her by further advice—of which the first dose had proved so useless—or to speed her departure. Ellinor broke on her meditations:

"You have always been so kind and good to me,—go on being so—please, do! Leave me alone now, dear Mrs. Forbes, for I cannot bear talking about it, and help me to go to-morrow, and you do not know how I will pray to God to bless you!"

Such an appeal was irresistible. Mrs. Forbes kissed her very tenderly, and went to rejoin her daughters, who were clustered together in their mother's bedroom awaiting her coming.

"Well, mamma, how is she? What does she say?"

"She is in a very excited state, poor thing! and has got so strong an impression that it is her duty to go back to England and do all she can for this wretched old man, that I am afraid we must not oppose her. I am afraid that she really must go on Thursday."

Although Mrs. Forbes secured the services of a travelling-maid, Dr. Livingstone insisted on accompanying Ellinor to England, and it would have required more energy than she possessed at this time to combat a resolution which both words and manner expressed as determined. She would much rather have travelled alone with her maid; she did not feel the need of the services he offered; but she was utterly listless and broken down; all her interest was centred in the thought of Dixon and his approaching trial, and perplexity as to the mode in which she must do her duty.

They embarked late that evening in the tardy *Santa Lucia*, and Ellinor immediately went to her berth. She was not sea-sick; that might possibly have lessened her mental sufferings, which all night long tormented her. High-perched in an upper berth, she did not like disturbing the other occupants of the cabin till daylight appeared. Then she descended and dressed, and went on deck; the vessel was just passing the rocky coast of Elba, and the sky was flushed with rosy light, that made the shadows on the island of the most exquisite purple. The sea still heaved with yesterday's storm, but the motion only added to the beauty of the sparkles and white foam that dimpled and curled on the blue waters. The air was delicious, after the closeness of the cabin, and Ellinor only wondered that more people were not on deck to enjoy it. One or two stragglers came up, time after time, and began pacing the deck. Dr. Livingstone came up before very long; but he seemed to have made a rule of not obtruding himself on Ellinor, excepting when he could be of some use. After a few words of common-place morning greeting, he, too, began to walk backwards and forwards, while Ellinor sat quietly watching the lovely island receding fast from her view—a beautiful vision never to be seen again by her mortal eyes.

Suddenly there was a shock and stound all over the vessel, her progress was stopped, and a rocking vibration was felt everywhere. The quarter-deck was filled with blasts of steam, which obscured everything. Sick people came rushing up out of their berths in strange undress; the steerage passengers—a motley and picturesque set of people, in many varieties of gay costume—took refuge on the quarter-deck, speaking loudly in all varieties of French and Italian *patois*. Ellinor stood up in silent, wondering dismay. Was the *Santa Lucia* going down on the great deep, and Dixon unaided in his peril? Dr. Livingstone was by her side in a moment. She could scarcely see him for the vapour, nor hear him for the roar of the escaping steam.

"Do not be unnecessarily frightened," he repeated, a little louder. "Some accident has occurred to the engines. I will go and make instant inquiry, and come back to you as soon as I can. Trust to me."

He came back to where she sat trembling.

"A part of the engine is broken, through the carelessness of these Neapolitan engineers; they say we must make for the nearest port—return to Civita, in fact."

"But Elba is not many miles away," said Ellinor. "If this steam were but away, you could see it still."

"And if we were landed there we might stay on the island for many days; no steamer touches there; but if we return to Civita, we shall be in time for the Sunday boat."

"Oh, dear, dear!" said Ellinor. "To-day is the second—Sunday will be the fourth—the assizes begin on the seventh; how miserably unfortunate!"

"Yes!" he said, "it is. And these things always appear so doubly unfortunate when they hinder our serving others! But it does not follow that because the assizes begin at Hellingford on the seventh, Dixon's trial will come on so soon. We may still get to Marseilles on Monday evening; on by diligence to Lyons; it will—it must, I fear, be Thursday, at the earliest, before we reach Paris—Thursday, the eighth—and I suppose you know of some exculpatory evidence that has to be hunted up?"

He added this unwillingly; for he saw that Ellinor was jealous of the secresy she had hitherto maintained as to her reasons for believing Dixon innocent; but he could not help thinking that she, a gentle, timid woman, unaccustomed to action or business, would require some of the assistance which he would have been so thankful to give her; especially as this untoward accident would increase the press of time in which what was to be done would have to be done.

But no. Ellinor scarcely replied to his half-inquiry as to her reasons for hastening to England. She yielded to all his directions, agreed to his plans, but gave him none of her confidence, and he had to submit to this exclusion from sympathy in the exact causes of her anxiety.

Once more in the dreary sala, with the gaudy painted ceiling, the bare dirty floor, the innumerable rattling doors and windows! Ellinor was submissive and patient in demeanour, because so sick and despairing at heart. Her maid was ten times as demonstrative of annoyance and disgust; she who had no particular reason for wanting to reach England, but who thought it became her dignity to make it seem as though she had.

At length the weary time was over; and again they sailed past Elba, and arrived at Marseilles. Now Ellinor began to feel how much assistance it was to her to have Dr. Livingstone for a "courier," as he had several times called himself.

CHAPTER XIV.

"Where now?" said the canon, as they approached the London Bridge station.

"To the Great Western," said she; "Hellingford is on that line, I see. But, please, now we must part."

"Then I may not go with you to Hellingford? At any rate, you will allow me to go with you to the railway station, and do my last office as courier in getting you your ticket and placing you in the carriage."

So they went together to the station, and learnt that no train was leaving for Hellingford for two hours. There was nothing for it but to go to the hotel close by, and pass away the time as best they could.

Ellinor called for her maid's accounts, and dismissed her. Some refreshment that the canon had ordered was eaten, and the table cleared. He began walking up and down the room, his arms folded, his eyes cast down. Every now and then he looked at the clock on the mantelpiece. When that showed that it only wanted a quarter of an hour to the time appointed for the train to start, he came up to Ellinor, who sat leaning her head upon her hand, her hand resting on the table.

"Miss Wilkins," he began—and there was something peculiar in his tone which startled Ellinor—"I am sure you will not scruple to apply to me if in any possible way I can help you in this sad trouble of yours?"

"No indeed I won't!" said Ellinor, gratefully, and putting out her hand as a token. He took it, and held it; she went on, a little more hastily than before: "You know you were so good as to say you would go at once and see Miss Monro, and tell her all you know, and that I will write to her as soon as I can."

"May I not ask for one line?" he continued, still holding her hand.

"Certainly: so kind a friend as you shall hear all I can tell; that is, all I am at liberty to tell."

"A friend! Yes, I am a friend; and I will not urge any other claim just now. Perhaps—"

Ellinor could not affect to misunderstand him. His manner implied even more than his words.

"No!" she said, eagerly. "We are friends. That is it. I think we shall always be friends, though I will tell you now—something—this much—it is a sad secret. God help me! I am as guilty as poor Dixon, if, indeed, he is guilty—but he is innocent—indeed he is!"

"If he is no more guilty than you, I am sure he is! Let me be more than your friend, Ellinor—let me know all, and help you all that I can, with the right of an affianced husband."

"No, no!" said she, frightened both at what she had revealed, and his eager, warm, imploring manner. "That can never be. You do not know the disgrace that may be hanging over me."

"If that is all," said he, "I take my risk—if that is all—if you only fear that I may shrink from sharing any peril you may be exposed to."

"It is not peril—it is shame and obloquy—" she murmured.

"Well! shame and obloquy. Perhaps, if I knew all I could shield you from it."

"Don't, pray, speak any more about it now; if you do, I must say 'No.'"

She did not perceive the implied encouragement in these words; but he did, and they sufficed to make him patient.

The time was up, and he could only render her his last services as "courier," and none other but the necessary words at starting passed between them.

But he went away from the station with a cheerful heart; while she, sitting alone and quiet, and at last approaching near to the place where so much was to be decided, felt sadder and sadder, heavier and heavier.

All the intelligence she had gained since she had seen the *Galignani* in Paris, had been from the waiter at the Great Western Hotel, who, after returning from a vain search for an unoccupied *Times*, had volunteered the information that there was an unusual demand for the paper because of Hellingford Assizes, and the trial there for murder that was going on.

There was no electric telegraph in those days; at every station Ellinor put her head out, and enquired if the murder trial at Hellingford was ended. Some porters told her one thing, some another, in their hurry; she felt that she could not rely on them.

"Drive to Mr. Johnson's in the High street—quick, quick. I will give you half-a-crown if you will go quick."

For, indeed, her endurance, her patience, was strained almost to snapping; yet at Hellingford station, where doubtless they could have told her the truth, she dared not ask the question. It was past eight o'clock at night. In many houses in the little country town there were unusual lights and sounds. The inhabitants were showing their hospitality to such of the strangers brought by the assizes, as were lingering there now that the business which had drawn them was over. The Judges had left the town that afternoon, to wind up the circuit by the short list of a neighbouring county town.

Mr. Johnson was entertaining a dinner-party of attorneys when he was summoned from dessert by the announcement of a "lady who wanted to speak to him immediate and particular."

He went into his study in not the best of tempers. There he found his client, Miss Wilkins, white and ghastly, standing by the fireplace, with her eyes fixed on the door.

"It is you, Miss Wilkins! I am very glad—"

"Dixon!" said she. It was all she could utter.

Mr. Johnson shook his head.

"Ah; that's a sad piece of business, and I'm afraid it has shortened your visit at Rome."

"Is he—?"

"Ay, I'm afraid there's no doubt of his guilt. At any rate, the jury found him guilty, and—"

"And!" she repeated, quickly, sitting down, the better to hear the words that she knew were coming—

"He is condemned to death."

"When?"

"The Saturday but one after the Judges left the town, I suppose—it's the usual time."

"Who tried him?"

"Judge Corbet; and, for a new judge, I must say I never knew one who got through his business so well. It was really as much as I could stand to hear him condemning the prisoner to death. Dixon was undoubtedly guilty, and he was as stubborn as could be—a sullen old fellow who would let no one help him through. I'm sure I did my best for him at Miss Monro's desire and for your sake. But he would furnish me with no particulars, help us to no evidence. I had the hardest work to keep him from confessing all before witnesses, who would have been bound to repeat it as evidence against him. Indeed, I never thought he would have pleaded 'Not Guilty.' I think it was only with a desire to justify himself in the eyes of some old Hamley acquaintances. Good God, Miss Wilkins! What's the matter? You're not fainting!" He rang the bell till the rope remained in his hands. "Here, Esther! Jerry! Whoever you are, come quick! Miss Wilkins has fainted! Water! Wine! Tell Mrs. Johnson to come here directly!"

Mrs. Johnson, a kind, motherly woman, who had been excluded from the "gentleman's dinner party," and had devoted her time to superintending the dinner her husband had ordered, came in answer to his call for assistance, and found Ellinor lying back in her chair white and senseless.

"Bessy, Miss Wilkins has fainted; she has had a long journey, and is in a fidget about Dixon, the old fellow who was sentenced to be hung for that murder, you know. I can't stop here, I must go back to those men. You bring her round, and see her to bed. The blue room is empty since Horner left. She must stop here, and I'll see her in the morning. Take care of her, and keep her mind as easy as you can, will you, for she can do no good by fidgeting."

And, knowing that he left Ellinor in good hands, and with plenty of assistance about her, he returned to his friends.

Ellinor came to herself before long.

"It was very foolish of me, but I could not help it," said she, apologetically.

"No; to be sure not, dear. Here, drink this; it is some of Mr. Johnson's best port wine that he has sent out on purpose for you. Or would you rather have some white soup—or what? We've had everything you could think of for dinner, and you've only to ask and have. And then you must go to bed, my dear—Mr. Johnson says you must; and there's a well-aired room, for Mr. Horner only left us this morning."

"I must see Mr. Johnson again, please."

"But indeed you must not. You must not worry your poor head with business now; and Johnson would only talk to you on business. No; go to bed, and sleep soundly, and then you'll get up quite bright and strong, and fit to talk about business."

"I cannot sleep—I cannot rest till I have asked Mr. Johnson one or two more questions; indeed I cannot," pleaded Ellinor.

Mrs. Johnson knew that her husband's orders on such occasions were peremptory, and that she should come in for a good conjugal scolding if, after what he had said, she ventured to send for him again. Yet Ellinor looked so entreating and wistful that she could hardly find in her heart to refuse her. A bright thought struck her.

"Here is pen and paper, my dear. Could you not write the questions you wanted to ask? and he'll just jot down the answers upon the same piece of paper. I'll send it in by Jerry. He has got friends to dinner with him, you see."

Ellinor yielded. She sat, resting her weary head on her hand, and wondering what were the questions which would have come so readily to her tongue could she have been face to face with him. As it was, she only wrote this:

"How early can I see you to-morrow morning? Will you take all the necessary steps for my going to Dixon as soon as possible? Could I be admitted to him to-night?"

The pencilled answers were:

"Eight o'clock. Yes. No."

"I suppose he knows best," said Ellinor, sighing, as she read the last word. "But it seems wicked in me to be going to bed—and he so near, in prison."

When she rose up and stood, she felt the former dizziness return, and that reconciled her to seeking rest before she entered upon the duties which were becoming clearer before her, now that she knew all and was on the scene of action. Mrs. Johnson brought her white-wine whey instead of the tea she had asked for; and perhaps it was owing to this that she slept so soundly.

CHAPTER XV.

When Ellinor awoke the clear light of dawn was fully in the room. She could not remember where she was; for so many mornings she had wakened up in strange places that it took her several minutes before she could make out the geographical whereabouts of the heavy blue moreen curtains, the print of the lord-lieutenant of the county on the wall, and all the handsome ponderous mahogany furniture that stuffed up the room. As soon as full memory came into her mind, she started up; nor did she go to bed again, although she saw by her watch on the dressing-table that it was not yet six o'clock. She dressed herself with the dainty completeness so habitual to her that it had become an unconscious habit, and then—the instinct was irrepressible—she put on her bonnet and shawl, and went down, past the servant on her knees cleaning the doorstep, out into the fresh open air; and so she found her way down the High Street to Hellingford Castle, the building in which the courts of assize were held—the prison in which Dixon lay condemned to die. She almost knew she could not see him; yet it seemed like some amends to her conscience for having slept through so many hours of the night if she made the attempt. She went up to the porter's lodge, and asked the little girl sweeping out the place if she might see Abraham Dixon. The child stared at her, and ran into the house, bringing out her father, a great burly man, who had not yet donned either coat or waistcoat, and who, consequently, felt the morning air as rather nipping. To him Ellinor repeated her question.

"Him as is to be hung come Saturday se'nnight? Why, ma'am, I've nought to do with it. You may go to the governor's house and try; but, if you'll excuse me, you'll have your walk for your pains. Them in the condemned cells is never seen by nobody without the sheriff's order. You may go up to the governor's house and welcome; but they'll only tell you the same. Yon's the governor's house."

Ellinor fully believed the man, and yet she went on to the house indicated, as if she still hoped that in her case there might be some exception to the rule, which she now remembered to have heard of before, in days when such a possible desire as to see a condemned prisoner was treated by her as a wish that some people might have, did have—people as far removed from her circle of circumstances as the inhabitants of the moon. Of course she met with the same reply, a little more abruptly given, as if every man was from his birth bound to know such an obvious regulation.

She went out past the porter, now fully clothed. He was sorry for her disappointment, but could not help saying, with a slight tone of exultation: "Well, you see I was right, ma'am!"

She walked as nearly round the castle as ever she could, looking up at the few high-barred windows she could see, and wondering in what part of the building Dixon was confined. Then she went into the adjoining churchyard, and sitting down upon a tombstone, she gazed idly at the view spread below her—a view which was considered as the lion of the place, to be shown to all strangers by the inhabitants of Hellingford. Ellinor did not see it, however; she only saw the blackness of that fatal night, the hurried work—the lanterns glancing to and fro. She only heard the hard breathing of those who are engaged upon unwonted labour; the few hoarse muttered words; the swaying of the branches to and fro. All at once the church clock above her struck eight, and then pealed out for distant labourers to cease their work for a time. Such was the old custom of the place. Ellinor rose up, and made her way back to Mr. Johnson's house in High Street. The room felt close and confined in which she awaited her interview with Mr. Johnson, who had sent down an apology for having overslept himself, and at last made his appearance in a hurried half-awakened state, in consequence of his late hospitality of the night before.

"I am so sorry I gave you all so much trouble last night," said Ellinor, apologetically. "I was overtired, and much shocked by the news I heard."

"No trouble, no trouble, I am sure. Neither Mrs. Johnson nor I felt it in the least a trouble. Many ladies I know feel such things very trying, though there are others that can stand a judge's putting on the black cap better than most men. I'm sure I saw some as composed as could be under Judge Corbet's speech."

"But about Dixon? He must not die, Mr. Johnson."

"Well, I don't know that he will," said Mr. Johnson, in something of the tone of voice he would have used in soothing a child. "Judge Corbet said something about the possibility of a pardon. The jury did not recommend him to mercy: you see, his looks went so much against him, and all the evidence was so strong, and no defence, so to speak, for he would not furnish any information on which we could base defence. But the judge did give some hope, to my mind, though there are others that think differently."

"I tell you, Mr. Johnson, he must not die, and he shall not. To whom must I go?"

"Whew! Have you got additional evidence?" with a sudden sharp glance of professional inquiry.

"Never mind," Ellinor answered. "I beg your pardon . . . only tell me into whose hands the power of life and death has passed."

"Into the Home Secretary's—Sir Phillip Homes; but you cannot get access to him on such an errand. It is the judge who tried the case that must urge a reprieve—Judge Corbet."

"Judge Corbet?"

"Yes; and he was rather inclined to take a merciful view of the whole case. I saw it in his charge. He'll be the person for you to see. I suppose you don't like to give me your confidence, or else I could arrange and draw up what will have to be said?"

"No. What I have to say must be spoken to the arbiter—to no one else. I am afraid I answered you impatiently just now. You must forgive me; if you knew all, I am sure you would."

"Say no more, my dear lady. We will suppose you have some evidence not adduced at the trial. Well; you must go up and see the judge, since you don't choose to impart it to any one, and lay it before him. He will doubtless compare it with his notes of the trial, and see how far it agrees with them. Of course you must be prepared with some kind of proof; for Judge Corbet will have to test your evidence."

"It seems strange to think of him as the judge," said Ellinor, almost to herself.

"Why, yes. He's but a young judge. You knew him at Hamley, I suppose? I remember his reading there with Mr. Ness."

"Yes, but do not let us talk more about that time. Tell me when can I see Dixon? I have been to the castle already, but they said I must have a sheriff's order."

"To be sure. I desired Mrs. Johnson to tell you so last night. Old Ormerod was dining here; he is clerk to the magistrates, and I told him of your wish. He said he would see Sir Henry Croper, and have the order here before ten. But all this time Mrs. Johnson is waiting breakfast for us. Let me take you into the dining-room."

It was very hard work for Ellinor to do her duty as a guest, and to allow herself to be interested and talked to on local affairs by her host and hostess. But she felt as if she had spoken shortly and abruptly to Mr. Johnson in their previous conversation, and that she must try and make amends for it; so she attended to all the details about the restoration of the church, and the difficulty of getting a good music-master for the three little Miss Johnsons, with all her usual gentle good breeding and patience, though no one can tell how her heart and imagination were full of the coming interview with poor old Dixon.

By-and-by Mr. Johnson was called out of the room to see Mr. Ormerod, and receive the order of admission from him. Ellinor clasped her hands tight together as she listened with apparent composure to Mrs Johnson's never-ending praise of the Hullah system. But when Mr. Johnson returned, she could not help interrupting her eulogy, and saying—

"Then I may go now?"

Yes, the order was there—she might go, and Mr. Johnson would accompany her, to see that she met with no difficulty or obstacle.

As they walked thither, he told her that some one—a turnkey, or some one—would have to be present at the interview; that such was always the rule in the case of condemned prisoners; but that if this third person was "obliging," he would keep out of earshot. Mr. Johnson quietly took care to see that the turnkey who accompanied Ellinor was "obliging."

The man took her across high-walled courts, along stone corridors, and through many locked doors, before they came to the condemned cells.

"I've had three at a time in here," said he, unlocking the final door, "after Judge Morton had been here. We always called him the 'Hanging Judge.' But its five years since he died, and now there's never more than one in at a time; though once it was a woman for poisoning her husband. Mary Jones was her name."

The stone passage out of which the cells opened was light, and bare, and scrupulously clean. Over each door was a small barred window, and an outer window of the same description was placed high up in the cell, which the turnkey now opened.

Old Abraham Dixon was sitting on the side of his bed, doing nothing. His head was bent, his frame sunk, and he did not seem to care to turn round and see who it was that entered.

Ellinor tried to keep down her sobs while the man went up to him, and laying his hand on his shoulder, and lightly shaking him, he said:

"Here's a friend come to see you, Dixon." Then, turning to Ellinor, he added, "There's some as takes it in this kind o' stunned way, while others are as restless as a wild beast in a cage, after they're sentenced." And then he withdrew into the passage, leaving the door open, so that he could see all that passed if he chose to look, but ostentatiously keeping his eyes averted, and whistling to himself, so that he could not hear what they said to each other.

Dixon looked up at Ellinor, but then let his eyes fall on the ground again; the increasing trembling of his shrunken frame was the only sign he gave that he had recognised her.

She sat down by him, and took his large horny hand in hers. She wanted to overcome her inclination to sob hysterically before she spoke. She stroked the bony shrivelled fingers, on which her hot scalding tears kept dropping.

"Dunnot do that," said he, at length, in a hollow voice. "Dunnot take on about it; it's best as it is, missy."

"No, Dixon, it's not best. It shall not be. You know it shall not—cannot be."

"I'm rather tired of living. It's been a great strain and labour for me. I think I'd as lief be with God as with men. And you see, I were fond on him ever sin' he were a little lad, and told me what hard times he had at school, he did, just as if I were his brother! I loved him next to Molly Greaves. Dear! and I shall see her again, I reckon, come next Saturday week! They'll think well on me, up there, I'll be bound; though I cannot say as I've done all as I should do here below."

"But, Dixon," said Ellinor, "you know who did this—this—"

"Guilty o' murder," said he. "That's what they called it. Murder! And that it never were, choose who did it."

"My poor, poor father did it. I am going up to London this afternoon; I am going to see the judge, and tell him all."

"Don't you demean yourself to that fellow, missy. It's him as left you in the lurch as soon as sorrow and shame came nigh you."

He looked up at her now, for the first time; but she went on as if she had not noticed those wistful, weary eyes.

"Yes! I shall go to him. I know who it is; and I am resolved. After all, he may be better than a stranger, for real help; and I shall never remember any—anything else, when I think of you, good faithful friend."

"He looks but a wizened old fellow in his grey wig. I should hardly ha' known him. I gave him a look, as much as to say, 'I could tell tales o' you, my lord judge, if I chose.' I don't know if he heeded me, though. I suppose it were for a sign of old acquaintance that he said he'd recommend me to mercy. But I'd sooner have death nor mercy, by long odds. Yon man out there says mercy means Botany Bay. It 'ud be like killing me by inches, that would. It would. I'd liefer go straight to Heaven, than live on among the black folk."

He began to shake again: this idea of transportation, from its very mysteriousness, was more terrifying to him than death. He kept on saying plaintively, "Missy, you'll never let 'em send me to Botany Bay; I couldn't stand that."

"No, no!" said she. "You shall come out of this prison, and go home with me to East Chester; I promise you you shall. I promise you. I don't yet quite know how, but trust in my promise. Don't fret about Botany Bay. If you go there, I go too. I am so sure you will not go. And you know if you have done anything against the law in concealing that fatal night's work, I did too, and if you are to be punished, I will be punished too. But I feel sure it will be right; I mean, as right as anything can be, with the recollection of that time present to us, as it must always be." She almost spoke these last words to herself. They sat on, hand in hand for a few minutes more in silence.

"I thought you'd come to me. I knowed you were far away in foreign parts. But I used to pray to God. 'Dear Lord God!' I used to say, 'let me see her again.' I told the chaplain as I'd begin to pray for repentance, at after I'd done praying that I might see you once again: for it just seemed to take all my strength to say those words as I've named. And I thought as how God knew what was in my heart better than I could tell Him: how I was main and sorry for all as I'd ever done wrong; I allays were, at after it was done; but I thought as no one could know how bitter-keen I wanted to see you."

Again they sank into silence. Ellinor felt as if she would fain be away and active in procuring his release; but she also perceived how precious her presence was to him; and she did not like to leave him a moment before the time allowed her. His voice had changed to a weak, piping old man's quaver, and between the times of his talking he seemed to relapse into a dreamy state; but through it all he held her hand tight, as though afraid that she would leave him.

So the hour elapsed, with no more spoken words than those above. From time to time Ellinor's tears dropped down upon her lap; she could not restrain them, though she scarce knew why she cried just then.

At length the turnkey said that the time allowed for the interview was ended. Ellinor spoke no word; but rose, and bent down and kissed the old man's forehead, saying—

"I shall come back to-morrow. God keep and comfort you!"

So almost without an articulate word from him in reply (he rose up, and stood on his shaking legs, as she bade him farewell, putting his hand to his head with the old habitual mark of respect), she went her way, swiftly out of the prison, swiftly back with Mr. Johnson to his house, scarcely patient or strong enough in her hurry to explain to him fully all that she meant to do. She only asked him a few absolutely requisite questions; and informed him of her intention to go straight to London to see Judge Corbet.

Just before the railway carriage in which she was seated started on the journey, she bent forward, and put out her hand once more to Mr. Johnson. "To-morrow I will thank you for all," she said. "I cannot now."

It was about the same time that she had reached Hellingford on the previous night, that she arrived at the Great Western station on this evening—past eight o'clock. On the way she had remembered and arranged many things: one important question she had omitted to ask Mr. Johnson; but that was easily remedied. She had not enquired where she could find Judge Corbet; if she had, Mr. Johnson could probably have given her his professional address. As it was, she asked for a Post-Office Directory at the hotel, and looked out for his private dwelling—128 Hyde Park Gardens.

She rang for a waiter.

"Can I send a messenger to Hyde Park Gardens?" she said, hurrying on to her business, tired and worn out as she was. "It is only to ask if Judge Corbet is at home this evening. If he is, I must go and see him."

The waiter was a little surprised, and would gladly have had her name to authorise the enquiry but she could not bear to send it: it would be bad enough that first meeting, without the feeling that he, too, had had time to recall all the past days. Better to go in upon him unprepared, and plunge into the subject.

The waiter returned with the answer while she yet was pacing up and down the room restlessly, nerving herself for the interview.

"The messenger has been to Hyde Park Gardens, ma'am. The Judge and Lady Corbet are gone out to dinner."

Lady Corbet! Of course Ellinor knew that he was married. Had she not been present at the wedding in East Chester Cathedral? But, somehow, these recent events had so carried her back to old times, that the intimate association of the names, "the Judge and Lady Corbet," seemed to awaken her out of some dream.

"Oh, very well," she said, just as if these thoughts were not passing rapidly through her mind. "Let me be called at seven to-morrow morning, and let me have a cab at the door to Hyde Park Gardens at eight."

And so she went to bed; but scarcely to sleep. All night long she had the scenes of those old times, the happy, happy days of her youth, the one terrible night that cut all happiness short, present before her. She could almost have fancied that she heard the long-silent sounds of her father's step, her father's way of breathing, the rustle of his newspaper as he hastily turned it over, coming through the lapse of years; the silence of the night. She knew that she had the little writing-case of her girlhood with her, in her box. The treasures of the dead that it contained, the morsel of dainty sewing, the little sister's golden curl, the half-finished letter to Mr. Corbet, were all there. She took them out, and looked at each separately; looked at them long—long and wistfully. "Will it be of any use to me?" she questioned of herself, as she was about to put her father's letter back into its receptacle. She read the last words over again, once more:

"From my death-bed I adjure you to stand her friend; I will beg pardon on my knees for anything."

"I will take it," thought she. "I need not bring it out; most likely there will be no need for it, after what I shall have to say. All is so altered, so changed between us, as utterly as if it never had been, that I think I shall have no shame in showing it him, for my own part of it. While, if he sees poor papa's, dear, dear papa's suffering humility, it may make him think more gently of one who loved him once though they parted in wrath with each other, I'm afraid."

So she took the letter with her when she drove to Hyde Park Gardens.

Every nerve in her body was in such a high state of tension that she could have screamed out at the cabman's boisterous knock at the door. She got out hastily, before any one was ready or willing to answer such an untimely summons; paid the man double what he ought to have had; and stood there, sick, trembling, and humble.

CHAPTER XVI AND LAST.

"Is Judge Corbet at home? Can I see him?" she asked of the footman, who at length answered the door.

He looked at her curiously, and a little familiarly, before he replied,

"Why, yes! He's pretty sure to be at home at this time of day; but whether he'll see you is quite another thing."

"Would you be so good as to ask him? It is on very particular business."

"Can you give me a card? your name, perhaps, will do, if you have not a card. I say, Simmons" (to a lady's-maid crossing the hall), "is the judge up yet?"

"Oh, yes! he's in his dressing-room this half-hour. My lady is coming down directly. It is just breakfast-time."

"Can't you put it off and come again, a little later?" said he, turning once more to Ellinor—white Ellinor! trembling Ellinor!

"No! please let me come in. I will wait. I am sure Judge Corbet will see me, if you will tell him I am here. Miss Wilkins. He will know the name."

"Well, then; will you wait here till I have got breakfast in?" said the man, letting her into the hall, and pointing to the bench there, he took her, from her dress, to be a lady's-maid or governess, or at most a tradesman's daughter; and, besides, he was behindhand with all his preparations. She came in and sat down.

"You will tell him I am here," she said faintly.

"Oh, yes, never fear: I'll send up word, though I don't believe he'll come to you before breakfast."

He told a page, who ran upstairs, and, knocking at the judge's door, said that a Miss Jenkins wanted to speak to him.

"Who?" asked the judge from the inside.

"Miss Jenkins. She said you would know the name, sir."

"Not I. Tell her to wait."

So Ellinor waited. Presently down the stairs, with slow deliberate dignity, came the handsome Lady Corbet, in her rustling silks and ample petticoats, carrying her fine boy, and followed by her majestic nurse. She was ill-pleased that any one should come and take up her husband's time when he was at home, and supposed to be enjoying domestic leisure; and her imperious, inconsiderate nature did not prompt her to any civility towards the gentle creature sitting down, weary and heart-sick, in her house. On the contrary, she looked her over as she slowly descended, till Ellinor shrank abashed from the steady gaze of the large black eyes. Then she, her baby and nurse, disappeared into the large dining-room, into which all the preparations for breakfast had been carried.

The next person to come down would be the judge. Ellinor instinctively put down her veil. She heard his quick decided step; she had known it well of old.

He gave one of his sharp, shrewd glances at the person sitting in the hall and waiting to speak to him, and his practised eye recognised the lady at once, in spite of her travel-worn dress.

"Will you just come into this room?" said he, opening the door of his study, to the front of the house: the dining-room was to the back; they communicated by folding-doors.

The astute lawyer placed himself with his back to the window; it was the natural position of the master of the apartment; but it also gave him the advantage of seeing his companion's face in full light. Ellinor lifted her veil; it had only been a dislike to a recognition in the hall which had made her put it down.

Judge Corbet's countenance changed more than hers; she had been prepared for the interview; he was not. But he usually had the full command of the expression on his face.

"Ellinor! Miss Wilkins! is it you?" And he went forwards, holding out his hand with cordial greeting, under which the embarrassment, if he felt any, was carefully concealed. She could not speak all at once in the way she wished.

"That stupid Henry told me 'Jenkins!' I beg your pardon. How could they put you down to sit in the hall? You must come in and have some breakfast with us; Lady Corbet will be delighted, I'm sure." His sense of the awkwardness of the meeting with the woman who was once to have been his wife, and of the probable introduction which was to follow to the woman who was his actual wife grew upon him, and made him speak a little hurriedly. Ellinor's next words were a wonderful relief; and her soft gentle way of speaking was like the touch of a cooling balsam.

"Thank you, you must excuse me. I am come strictly on business, otherwise I should never have thought of calling on you at such an hour. It is about poor Dixon."

"Ah! I thought as much!" said the judge, handing her a chair, and sitting down himself. He tried to compose his mind to business, but in spite of his strength of character, and his present efforts, the remembrance of old times would come back at the sound of her voice. He wondered if he was as much changed in appearance as she struck him as being in that first look of recognition; after that first glance he rather avoided meeting her eyes.

"I knew how much you would feel it. Some one at Hellingford told me you were abroad, in Rome, I think. But you must not distress yourself unnecessarily; the sentence is sure to be commuted to transportation, or something equivalent. I was talking to the Home Secretary about it only last night. Lapse of time and subsequent good character quite preclude any idea of capital punishment." All the time that he said this he had other thoughts at the back of his mind—some curiosity, a little regret, a touch of remorse, a wonder how the meeting (which, of course, would have to be some time) between Lady Corbet and Ellinor would go off; but he spoke clearly enough on the subject in hand, and no outward mark of distraction from it appeared.

Ellinor answered:

"I came to tell you, what I suppose may be told to any judge, in confidence and full reliance on his secrecy, that Abraham Dixon was not the murderer." She stopped short, and choked a little.

The judge looked sharply at her.

"Then you know who was?" said he.

"Yes," she replied, with a low, steady voice, looking him full in the face, with sad, solemn eyes.

The truth flashed into his mind. He shaded his face, and did not speak for a minute or two. Then he said, not looking up, a little hoarsely, "This, then, was the shame you told me of long ago?"

"Yes," said she.

Both sat quite still; quite silent for some time. Through the silence a sharp, clear voice was heard speaking through the folding-doors.

"Take the kedgeree down, and tell the cook to keep it hot for the judge. It is so tiresome people coming on business here, as if the judge had not his proper hours for being at chambers."

He got up hastily, and went into the dining-room; but he had audibly some difficulty in curbing his wife's irritation.

When he came back, Ellinor said:

"I am afraid I ought not to have come here now."

"Oh! it's all nonsense!" said he, in a tone of annoyance. "You've done quite right." He seated himself where he had been before; and again half covered his face with his hand.

"And Dixon knew of this. I believe I must put the fact plainly—to you—your father was the guilty person? he murdered Dunster?"

"Yes. If you call it murder. It was done by a blow, in the heat of passion. No one can ever tell how Dunster always irritated papa," said Ellinor, in a stupid, heavy way; and then she sighed.

"How do you know this?" There was a kind of tender reluctance in the judge's voice, as he put all these questions. Ellinor had made up her mind beforehand that something like them must be asked, and must also be answered; but she spoke like a sleep-walker.

"I came into papa's room just after he had struck Mr. Dunster the blow. He was lying insensible, as we thought—dead, as he really was."

"What was Dixon's part in it? He must have known a good deal about it. And the horse-lancet that was found with his name upon it?"

"Papa went to wake Dixon, and he brought his fleam—I suppose to try and bleed him. I have said enough, have I not? I seem so confused. But I will answer any question to make it appear that Dixon is innocent."

The judge had been noting all down. He sat still now without replying to her. Then he wrote rapidly, referring to his previous paper, from time to time. In five minutes or so he read the facts which Ellinor had stated, as he now arranged them, in a legal and connected form. He just asked her one or two trivial questions as he did so. Then he read it over to her, and asked her to sign it. She took up the pen, and held it, hesitating.

"This will never be made public?" said she.

"No; I shall take care that no one but the Home Secretary sees it."

"Thank you. I could not help it, now it has come to this."

"There are not many men like Dixon," said the judge, almost to himself, as he sealed the paper in an envelope.

"No," said Ellinor; "I never knew any one so faithful."

And just at the same moment the reflection on a less faithful person that these words might seem to imply struck both of them, and each instinctively glanced at the other.

"Ellinor!" said the judge, after a moment's pause, "we are friends, I hope?"

"Yes; friends," said she, quietly and sadly.

He felt a little chagrined at her answer. Why, he could hardly tell. To cover any sign of his feeling he went on talking.

"Where are you living now?"

"At East Chester."

"But you come sometimes to town, don't you? Let us know always—whenever you come; and Lady Corbet shall call on you. Indeed, I wish you'd let me bring her to see you to-day."

"Thank you. I am going straight back to Hellingford; at least, as soon as you can get me the pardon for Dixon."

He half smiled at her ignorance.

"The pardon must be sent to the sheriff, who holds the warrant for his execution. But, of course, you may have every assurance that it shall be sent as soon as possible. It is just the same as if he had it now."

"Thank you very much," said Ellinor rising.

"Pray don't go without breakfast. If you would rather not see Lady Corbet just now, it shall be sent in to you in this room, unless you have already breakfasted."

"No, thank you; I would rather not. You are very kind, and I am very glad to have seen you once again. There is just one thing more," said she, colouring a little and hesitating. "This note to you was found under papa's pillow after his death; some of it refers to past things; but I should be glad if you could think as kindly as you can of poor papa—and so—if you will read it—"

He took it and read it, not without emotion. Then he laid it down on his table, and said—

"Poor man! he must have suffered a great deal for that night's work. And you, Ellinor, you have suffered, too."

Yes, she had suffered; and he who spoke had been one of the instruments of her suffering, although he seemed forgetful of it. She shook her head a little for reply. Then she looked up at him—they were both standing at the time—and said:

"I think I shall be happier now. I always knew it must be found out. Once more, good-by, and thank you. I may take this letter, I suppose?" said she, casting envious loving eyes at her father's note, lying unregarded on the table.

"Oh! certainly, certainly," said he; and then he took her hand; he held it, while he looked into her face. He had thought it changed when he had first seen her, but it was now almost the same to him as of yore. The sweet shy eyes, the indicated dimple in the cheek, and something of fever had brought a faint pink flush into her usually colourless cheeks. Married judge though he was, he was not sure if she had not more charms for him still in her sorrow and her shabbiness than the handsome stately wife in the next room, whose looks had not been of the pleasantest when he left her a few minutes before. He sighed a little regretfully as Ellinor went away. He had obtained the position he had struggled for, and sacrificed for; but now he could not help wishing that the slaughtered creature laid on the shrine of his ambition were alive again.

The kedgeree was brought up again, smoking hot, but it remained untasted by him; and though he appeared to be reading the *Times*, he did not see a word of the distinct type. His wife, meanwhile, continued her complaints of the untimely visitor, whose name he did not give to her in its corrected form, as he was not anxious that she should have it in her power to identify the call of this morning with a possible future acquaintance.

When Ellinor reached Mr. Johnson's house in Hellingford that afternoon, she found Miss Monro was there, and that she had been with much difficulty restrained by Mr. Johnson from following her to London.

Miss Monro fondled and purred inarticulately through her tears over her recovered darling, before she could speak intelligibly enough to tell her that Canon Livingstone had come straight to see her immediately on his return to East Chester, and had suggested her journey to Hellingford, in order that she might be of all the comfort she could to Ellinor. She did not at first let out that he had accompanied her to Hellingford; she was a little afraid of Ellinor's displeasure at his being there; Ellinor had always objected so much to any advance towards intimacy with him that Miss Monro had wished to make. But Ellinor was different now.

"How white you are, Nelly!" said Miss Monro. "You have been travelling too much and too fast, my child."

"My head aches!" said Ellinor, wearily. "But I must go to the castle, and tell my poor Dixon that he is reprieved—I am so tired! Will you ask Mr. Johnson to get me leave to see him? He will know all about it."

She threw herself down on the bed in the spare room; the bed with the heavy blue curtains. After an unheeded remonstrance, Miss Monro went to do her bidding. But it was now late afternoon, and Mr. Johnson said that it would be impossible for him to get permission from the sheriff that night.

"Besides," said he, courteously, "one scarcely knows whether Miss Wilkins may not give the old man false hopes—whether she has not been excited to have false hopes herself; it might be a cruel kindness to let her see him, without more legal certainty as to what his sentence, or reprieve, is to be. By to-morrow morning, if I have properly understood her story, which was a little confused—"

"She is so dreadfully tired, poor creature," put in Miss Monro, who never could bear the shadow of a suspicion that Ellinor was not wisest, best, in all relations and situations of life.

Mr. Johnson went on, with a deprecatory bow: "Well, then—it really is the only course open to her besides—persuade her to rest for this evening. By to-morrow morning I will have obtained the sheriff's leave, and he will most likely have heard from London."

"Thank you! I believe that will be best."

"It is the only course," said he.

When Miss Monro returned to the bedroom, Ellinor was in a heavy feverish slumber; so feverish and so uneasy did she appear, that, after the hesitation of a moment or two, Miss Monro had no scruple in wakening her.

But she did not appear to understand the answer to her request; she did not seem even to remember that she had made any request.

The journey to England, the misery, the surprises, had been too much for her. The morrow morning came, bringing the formal free pardon for Abraham Dixon. The sheriff's order for her admission to see the old man lay awaiting her wish to use it; but she knew nothing of all this.

For days, nay weeks, she hovered between life and death, tended, as of old, by Miss Monro, while good Mrs. Johnson was ever willing to assist.

One summer evening in early June she wakened into memory, Miss Monro heard the faint piping voice, as she kept her watch by the bedside.

"Where is Dixon?" asked she.

"At the canon's house at Bromham." This was the name of Dr. Livingstone's county parish.

"Why?"

"We thought it better to get him into country air and fresh scenes at once."

"How is he?"

"Much better. Get strong, and he shall come to see you."

"You are sure all is right?" said Ellinor.

"Sure, my dear. All is quite right."

Then Ellinor went to sleep again out of very weakness and weariness.

From that time she recovered pretty steadily. Her great desire was to return to East Chester as soon as possible. The associations of grief, anxiety, and coming illness, connected with Hellingford, made her wish to be once again in the solemn, quiet, sunny close of East Chester.

Canon Livingstone came over to assist Miss Monro in managing the journey with her invalid. But he did not intrude himself upon Ellinor, any more than he had done in coming from home.

The morning after her return, Miss Monro said:

"Do you feel strong enough to see Dixon?"

"Is he here?"

"He is at the canon's house. He sent for him from Bromham, in order that he might be ready for you to see him when you wished."

"Please let him come directly," said Ellinor, flushing and trembling.

She went to the door to meet the tottering old man; she led him to the easy-chair that had been placed and arranged for herself; she knelt down before him, and put his hands on her head, he trembling and shaking all the while.

"Forgive me all the shame and misery, Dixon. Say you forgive me; and give me your blessing. And then let never a word of the terrible past be spoken between us."

"It's not for me to forgive you, as never did harm to no one—"

"But say you do—it will ease my heart."

"I forgive thee!" said he. And then he raised himself to his feet with effort, and, standing up above her, he blessed her solemnly.

After that he sat down, she by him, gazing at him.

"Yon's a good man, missy," he said, at length, lifting his slow eyes and looking at her. "Better nor t'other ever was."

"He is a good man," said Ellinor.

But no more was spoken on the subject. The next day, Canon Livingstone made his formal call. Ellinor would fain have kept Miss Monro in the room, but that worthy lady knew better than to stop.

They went on, forcing talk on indifferent subjects. At last he could speak no longer on everything but that which he had most at heart. "Miss Wilkins!" (he had got up, and was standing by the mantelpiece, apparently examining the ornaments upon it)—"Miss Wilkins! is there any chance of your giving me a favourable answer now—you know what I mean—what we spoke about at the Great Western Hotel, that day?"

Ellinor hung her head.

"You know that I was once engaged before?"

"Yes! I know; to Mr. Corbet—he that is now the judge; you cannot suppose that would make any difference, if that is all. I have loved you, and you only, ever since we met, eighteen years ago. Miss Wilkins—Ellinor—put me out of suspense."

"I will!" said she, putting out her thin white hand for him to take and kiss, almost with tears of gratitude, but she seemed frightened at his impetuosity, and tried to check him. "Wait—you have not heard all—my poor, poor father, in a fit of anger, irritated beyond his bearing, struck the blow that killed Mr. Dunster—Dixon and I knew of it, just after the blow was struck—we helped to hide it—we kept the secret—my poor father died of sorrow and remorse—you now know all—can you still love me? It seems to me as if I had been an accomplice in such a terrible thing!"

"Poor, poor Ellinor!" said he, now taking her in his arms as a shelter. "How I wish I had known of all this years and years ago: I could have stood between you and so much!"

Those who pass through the village of Bromham, and pause to look over the laurel-hedge that separates the rectory garden from the road, may often see, on summer days, an old, old man, sitting in a wicker-chair, out upon the lawn. He leans upon his stick, and seldom raises his bent head; but for all that his eyes are on a level with the two little fairy children who come to him in all their small joys and sorrows, and who learnt to lisp his name almost as soon as they did that of their father and mother.

Nor is Miss Monro often absent; and although she prefers to retain the old house in the Close for winter quarters, she generally makes her way across to Canon Livingstone's residence every evening.

THE END

9 781835 528938